BRADD CHAMBERS

OUR JILLY

BRADD CHAMBERS

Our Jilly
Copyright © Bradd Chambers 2017
Published in 2017 by Bradd Chambers

Front cover slightly altercated. Original © Copyright Harlandspinksphotos / Creative Commons / Flickr: https://www.flickr.com/photos/mancake/1755267234/

BRADD CHAMBERS

Other publications from Bradd Chambers:

'*Someone Else's Life*'
Released June 2017
Available now on Amazon

BRADD CHAMBERS

Long before James Kingston was struck with the juvenile trials and tribulations of being a teenager... Exams, girlfriends, fighting to prove his innocence in a murder investigation... There was another disaster that tainted the minds of those residing in the small town of Rong Valley. A tragedy that claimed someone else's life. And it all began in 2007. With one girl. A little girl named Jill Yates..

BRADD CHAMBERS

CHAPTER 1:

Kane shivers in his thin white vest. His thrown-on trainers crunching on the ground. His little girl slung over his shoulder. He passes several neighbouring doors before letting her fall from his arms, getting a small satisfaction from the tiny splat that ricochets through the darkness as she hits the ground. There she is now. Where she belongs. With the moss and the insects and the damp. Sniffing and taking one last sweep of the alley, he lights a cigarette, temporarily illuminating the blackness, before returning home.

The metal bolt of the back gate whines into place as he has a mini battle getting the rusty key out. He turns to look in the window, deciding to finish his fag in peace. The living room is engulfed in the light from the massive, ugly glass shade that Donna's mum had bought them for a wedding present. The reds and greens give the room a sickly Christmassy feel that Kane can't stomach.

"Don't turn that bloody light on," Kane had barked at her on his way out.

"I need to clean up, I can barely see with that UV light."

Kane watches her scrubbing the tainted wooden floor. He glances through the window on his right to see the washing machine vibrating with life, the stained rug turning the soap a pinkish colour. Like her room. He can hear their youngest sobbing from the open window facing out into their small yard. He gazes up at the blinds swaying in the chilly March breeze. Clenching his jaw, he slams the back door shut. Kane charges down the hallway, but Donna stands in his way between the living room and the stairs.

"Just leave it now, will ya?"

But he doesn't stop. As he reaches her, he smacks her across the face, making her fall backwards into the living room and slide along the floor, still wet from the cleaning products that are burning into the woodwork. He climbs the stairs two at a time and comes to a halt outside her room. All is silent. She must've heard the commotion downstairs. Pressing his ear against the door, Kane can faintly hear her hiccups penetrate through the old faded wood.

"Go to sleep, Clara. Now!"

CHAPTER 2:

Toby has been barking for five minutes, and it sounds like he has no intention of stopping. Dylan rolls over and faces away from the light protruding through the window, wrapping an arm around his wife.

"Stupid dog," she groans, stroking his bare arm. "Your turn."

"You jokin'? I fed him yesterday."

"He must be wanting to pee."

"He's already outside. Bobby must've let him out before school."

"A walk then."

"It's only gone eight. He can hold his horses."

"Fine. I'll do it in a while. Have to go grab something for dinner anyway."

Mandy swings her legs out of bed and yawns, both arms in the air in a stretch. Dylan peels one eye open to see the arch in her back and slides his hands up her top, his old Beatles t-shirt.

13

"Oi," she laughs, pushing him away. Dylan moans and grabs her by the waist, forcing her back down on the bed. They start playfighting and kissing.

Still Toby barks.

Mandy climbs on top of him, continuing to kiss down his body until she slips his boxers off. Dylan groans with pleasure, but moments later, she suddenly stops. He looks down towards her. She's wearing a face of disgust, her hand still around him.

"I'm sorry, I can't concentrate with that dog."

Dylan can feel himself getting softer.

"Don't think about him. I'm not… Or wasn't."

"Just go down and see what he wants. Please?"

"Are you serious, Mand?"

"His barking is driving me insane. I can't think straight."

Dylan sighs and pulls on his jeans, tucking himself into them as delicately as he can without rubbing the zip.

"What's wrong, cock-block?" he says as he opens the back door.

Usually Toby is very obedient. Great with Bobby and the other neighbourhood kids. Smart as anything. But now, he's greeted with Toby's backside in the air, his nose trying to bury itself between the bottom of their back gate and the ground.

"What's the matter with ya?"

Toby spins around, sprints over and jumps up. Dylan goes to pet him, but he's back at the gate again in a heartbeat, barking louder. He scratches at it, whimpering.

"What is it, buddy?"

Dylan reaches for the padlock and flicks it around, pushing the gate. As it slides open, Toby escapes the yard as soon as the slit is wide enough for him to fit through. Dylan takes a look up and down the alley, before resting his eyes on the ground beside Toby.

"What the-"

CHAPTER 3:

"Come on, Kyra. We're going to be late!"

Helen Dawson plasters the jam on the wheaten bread, the only thing Kyra will eat, before popping it into the Hannah Montana lunch box. Kyra dances into the room, singing that annoying new Mika song.

"Mummy, why can't I get the bus into school like Alicia?"

"Because Alicia's going to big school, Kyra. You know that."

"But when can I go to big school with her?"

"In a few years."

"Ha! Like I'd be seen caught dead with her if she makes it to RV High."

Alicia storms into the room, her fringe covering most of her face, charging towards the front door.

"Bye, Mum."

"Alicia, your breakfast."

Alicia walks backwards, grabs a slice of toast from the island and shoves it into her mouth before spluttering out some inaudible thanks.

"Wait a sec."

Helen marches over and spins Alicia around. Through the piece of bread, Helen's shocked to see Alicia wearing silver sparkly eye shadow and eyeliner so dark, it looks like she hasn't slept in weeks.

"Do you really think your father will let you leave the house looking like that?"

"Looking like what?"

Detective Inspector Donald Dawson slops down the stairs and looks over at the couple half-heartedly. Upon inspecting Alicia's face, he snorts.

"I've arrested hookers with half as much make-up as that, up them stairs."

"But, Dad-"

"No buts."

Alicia clenches her fists and stamps her foot, letting out an exasperated groan, before storming back up the stairs, banging her feet loudly on every step on her ascent. The detective watches her, shaking his head as he bites into his wife's butter-soaked toast.

"Don't forget that Kyra needs collected at two today, not three. Okay, Don?"

Helen hobbles over in her heels before smacking a massive kiss on Dawson's cheek.

"Love you, hon."

BRADD CHAMBERS

The front door slams and, almost as if on cue, the radio in Alicia's room blares into life, turned up at full volume. Dawson sighs and fills his coffee cup, not yet ready to deal with his middle daughter. Give him an addict, burglar or pathological liar any day, but teenage girls were not his strong point. He'd already gotten Sue through her turbulent years, currently living the life of luxury in some dive in London. But that's where she wanted to go for university, and Dawson had to respect that. Only a few more years left before Alicia would, hopefully, come to her senses, but then they had Kyra to worry about.

Dawson's phone vibrates violently on the table. It's Jade.

"DS Simpson, how are you?"

"Fine, sir. But we need you in Promised Hill right away."

Dawson groans and pours the last of his coffee down the sink.

"What is it now? Drugs? Theft? Assault?"

"Er… No, sir. Meet me at 53 Windsor Place. It's urgent. A body has been found."

CHAPTER 4:

Dylan and Mandy Gardener are sitting hand-in-hand on their grubby lounge settee, waiting for DI Dawson. DS Jade Simpson stands talking to the forensics team before making her way through the carnage towards them.

"I'm really sorry that we've had to take over your whole house like this."

"No, don't worry. We'll do whatever needs to be done," Mandy sits forward, her eyes penetrating into Simpson's. Two mothers, only being able to imagine how awful this situation is.

"Did you say you knew the victim?"

"Yeah, she's Jill Yates. Lives around the corner," Dylan chips in. "She runs about with our Bobby."

Simpson writes on her pad.

"And you're sure it's her?"

"Positive. It was hard to tell at first, she was in such bad shape. But it's definitely her. She's been around here thousands of times."

A moments silence as Simpson takes note of his statement.

"DS Simpson, is she…"

Simpson looks up and gives Mandy a sombre nod.

"We tried everything we could. But they think she's been dead for hours. God only knows how long she's been lying in that alley. I guess it's rarely used?"

"Not very often. We use it to bring our bins back in every Wednesday. I've hardly ever seen anyone else using it," Dylan shakes his head.

"And the alley is used by…"

"All the houses on this row of Windsor Place, as well as the next street up, Connolly's Estate. All the houses on the left-hand side as you turn in."

"And everyone who lives in these houses would have access to the alley?"

"Yeah, we got given keys when we moved in."

"Anyone else?"

Dylan shrugs.

"Erm… The bin men, I'm guessing? And the council?"

Simpson's phone vibrates in her pocket, she smiles and stands. Dawson is shouting down the phone before she can even greet him.

"Whatever you do, do not step outside!"

"Sir?"

"The media have already got wind. There's only a few so far, but the whole place is still cordoned off. I've had to park down the street. I'm nearly there. Keep everyone inside."

Simpson flips down her mobile and lets everyone know that they're under house arrest until the big boss gets here. Moments later, Dawson thunders in through the front door, shaking off the light drizzle, and marches up to Simpson.

"Where is she?"

"The body still hasn't been moved, sir."

Dawson trots through the kitchen and into the tiny yard, only to be met with an army of white lab coats.

"Sorry, sir. But we can't contaminate the scene more than we may already have," a woman with a blue mask holds out a gloved hand.

"What do you mean '*more than we already have*?'"

"It was the dog that found her, sir," she nudges her head upwards towards the upstairs window, where the faint sound of a dog barking can be heard. "We're worried he may have moved the body or obstructed evidence. We've tried our best to preserve everything, but with the wind and the rain, and not knowing for sure how long she's been lying there, it's hard to judge."

21

Dawson curses before stomping back into the living room.

"The couple who live here seem to know the girl. Jill Yates, they've said." Simpson whispers in Dawson's ear. "Lives on the next street up."

Dawson stares at the mouldy skirting boards and grimaces. He hates Promised Hill.

"Have we had a positive ID for the body from a parent or guardian?"

"No, sir. But-"

"Then we can't say for certain. Have there been any missing children cases filed this morning?"

"No, sir. Should we go and speak to the Yates'?"

Dawson blows out and glares over at the house's tenants, whispering to each other on the sofa.

"Bit of an odd-looking couple, don't you think?"

"Sir?"

"I'm just saying. They seemed to know who she was instantly... Strange."

"Their boy went to school with her. They were friends."

"Yeah? Well we'll see about that.

CHAPTER 5:

The chiming of the doorbell at 52 Connolly's Estate echoes around the house, making Donna jump with fright. She turns off the UV light, gives the coffee table a quick brush with her hand and looks at herself in the cracked mirror. Fixing her dress, she tries to calm her breathing. Stepping forward to the front door, she opens it timidly, peering her head around the frame.

"Yes?"

A bald man in a smart suit stands before her, with a ginger middle-aged woman at his heels. Behind her, she sees a few uniformed police officers.

"Donna Yates?"

Donna nods, trying to hide her trembling hands.

"My name is Detective Inspector Donald Dawson. This is Detective Sergeant Jade Simpson. May we come in?"

Donna stands trembling as the two detectives flash their ID badges. She mentally pictures her entire house, top to bottom, wondering if there's anything on show. Anything to incriminate herself or her husband. Content that she's either used or stowed away the majority, she opens the door a fraction, before scurrying off to the living room. Sitting on *his* arm chair, she covers the burn mark with a dirty cushion. Dawson and Simpson flounce themselves down on the sofa opposite her.

"May I ask where your husband is, Donna?"

"He's at work. Down the bookies at the top of David's Lane."

"Could you get in contact with him and let him know he is to come home. Immediately. It's very important."

Donna nods, imagining the burn mark bursting to life as a flame once again as soon as she stands up and hobbles over to the phone in the hall.

"Dave's Bookies."

"Hi, Dave. Is Kane there?"

"Depends who's asking."

"His wife. It's very impor-"

The phone cuts out.

Donna curses in a hushed whisper as she trudges back into the living room, constantly fixing her dress out of nerves.

"Erm… They said he can't come to the phone. Must be really busy."

Dawson purses his lips and lifts a radio to his mouth.

"Greene, we need someone to go down the road to David's Lane. Dave's Bookies. Ask for..." he cuts off the transmission. "Sorry, what's your husband's name again?"

"Kane."

A flicker of recognition comes across Dawson's face.

"Kane Yates. Bring him here immediately."

"Rodger that, sir."

Dawson gazes around the dull room, not a picture in sight.

"I know that name... Kane Yates. Kane Yates. Do you have a photograph of him?"

Donna looks perplexed. Muttering to herself, she shuffles off into the hall in search of a recent photo of Kane. Dawson leans into Simpson's ear.

"She hasn't mentioned anything about Jill."

"She might not know."

"I thought you said forensics believe that she's been dead for several hours."

"They do."

"Well, would she not have reported her as a missing person?"

"Maybe she crept out of bed. At this stage, we know nothing."

Simpson shuts up quickly as Donna comes back into the room, handing over a picture of Kane with a few of the boys down the pub, all dressed in football tops and waving a flag.

"That's the only recent one I have, I'm afraid. Taken nearly two years ago."

Dawson nods and doesn't need to ask which one Kane is. He recognises him immediately. He's standing on the left with a pint to his lips. Their grandads are cousins. Or something along those lines. A far out relative of some sorts. Dawson remembers meeting him at a family party, probably coming up to twenty years ago. They hadn't talked much, but Dawson's heart now goes out to him.

"Mrs Yates, I'm sorry to intrude like this," Dawson sets the photograph on the filthy coffee table. "But we're here to talk about your daughter, Jill."

The wife winces.

"Oh?"

"Have you seen her today?"

"Yes. No… Let me think. Er… No, I heard her though. Leaving for school this morning."

"Definitely her?"

"Yes."

They had already contacted the school. Jill had not shown up for morning register.

"Do you have any other children?"

"Yes, Clara."

"Could it have been her you heard?"

"No, she's not very loud. Keeps herself to herself," she gives a nervous laugh.

That's when Dawson sees her hands. They squirm and fidget on her lap, despite her trying to clasp them together. He looks around at the room again. This doesn't look like a family home. Nothing like the Gardener's. He wouldn't say their house was particularly nice, but at least the Gardeners made an effort. This house looks like it's barely lived in. He takes a deep sniff and instantly recognises that someone was smoking weed here recently. It clings to the walls and refuses to leave.

"Mrs Yates, I-"

"Now, what's all this?"

The party of three look up to Kane, looking a bit heavier than the photograph, hobbling into the room.

"A police escort and everything. What am I? The bleedin' Queen?"

"Mr Yates," Dawson stands and extends his hand to Kane. Kane looks from the detective's hand to his face with a snarl.

"Why do you look familiar?"

"Donald Dawson. Detective Inspector. But you may know me a bit better as Ed and Natalie's kid? You're Emmet's son, right?"

Kane eyes the detective suspiciously.

"We're cousins. Well… Sort of. I met you at a party… Pfft… Must be nearly twenty years ag-"

"The Good Flowers Hotel?"

Dawson smiles.

"Yes. There."

Kane's defensive demeaner disappears and he pulls the detective in for a hug.

"How are you, man?"

"I'm fine. But look, that isn't why I'm here. Would you like to take a seat?"

Donna smiles timidly as Kane plonks himself down on the armrest beside her, the pillow falling onto the dirty floor.

"Look, we're here to talk about your daughter, Jill. Did you see her before work?"

Kane's smile hasn't lifted.

"No, I only started at ten there, so our paths didn't cross. Why? What has she done now?"

"Kane… Donna… There's no easy way to say this. But a girl was found in the alleyway behind your house. The body is currently being examined, but we've been told that the description of the girl fits the profile of your daughter, Jill. Of course, I'll need someone to formally identify the body before we are one hundred percent sure... But a neighbour seems certain that it is her. I'm so very sorry."

Kane's smile finally fades, being replaced with a half-open mouth. After a few seconds, the couple look at each other in confusion. Silent tears drip down Donna's face before Kane jumps up from his seat, making Donna grab for the pillow and push it against the spot where he was sitting, but not before Dawson steals a glimpse at the black burn etched into the sofa.

"This... This isn't possible," Kane's doing laps of the tiny room, which doesn't take very long.

"We need you to come with us to confirm whether it *is*, in fact, Jill. Your wife seems to be adamant that she heard Jill leave the house this morning. However, forensics believe that the body had been lying in that alley for several hours. If it turns out that it isn't Jill, then we have a lot more digging to do than we thought."

Kane snaps his head towards Donna, one eyebrow raised in confusion.

"I'll go. You stay here, darling."

CHAPTER 6:

"That's her."

Dawson can see Kane's reflection in the glass as he looks into the brightly lit room. Jill's young face protruding out from a single white sheet. Kane turns to Dawson, his chin quivering.

"That's my little girl."

"I'm so very sorry, Kane."

Kane pushes past him and into the hall, taking a seat on the metal chair mainly reserved for family members. He spreads his legs, digs his elbows into his knees and hides his face with his hands.

"I just want you to know that we are going to do everything in our power to catch your daughter's killer."

Kane nods, thanking the detectives, before standing. He mutters something about wanting to be alone, before exiting the morgue. Simpson's head snaps between Dawson and the swinging door.

"Sir?"

"Yes, Simpson?"

"We haven't taken statements. Nothing."

"I know, Simpson. We'll give him an hour to clear his head and then we'll go. Just give the family time to process this."

"But that's n-"

"I know it's not protocol, Simpson. But how often does something like this happen around here? That's my flesh and blood lying in there. He's clearly distraught."

"This killer is still at large, Dawson."

"And I know that. But they-"

"The longer we leave it, the more chance there is of someone else getting hurt, sir."

"They didn't even know the girl was missing, Simpson. Never mind dead. There's nothing of worth coming from their statements. Now give it until after lunch and we'll head back around. That's an order, okay?"

CHAPTER 7:

Roberta Holmes beams at the plaque above her cubicle. '*Crime Editor*.' She still can't believe it. Usually it's just measly GBHs or drugs around here, but now? Mere weeks later and she's got her first juicy murder case.

She's just back from the crime scene. No one was saying anything. Not even DI Dawson agreed to a statement, despite the increasing number of press and onlookers making his job a lot harder. She has come to know Promised Hill like the back of her hand. Every side street and shortcut. It's a hub for all things criminal in the town. If anything ever comes through, story wise, it sure as hell will be on one of those streets.

The body has just been moved, so once all manners of police are gone, she'll try and make contact with the people who discovered the body, believed to be a couple with a kid, by what some of the bystanders were saying.

"Any luck with Windsor Place then?"

Budds hobbles over to her desk, his mobile a short distance from his head.

"No, nothing. No statements or anything."

"Well, I want you to find out who has been killed, who has rung it in and what the police are doing about it. Ask some neighbours, get to know the community. You never know when it could come in handy."

"You're the boss."

Roberta sighs and picks up her bag, retreating down the corridor towards the back carpark. He couldn't have just rung to save her the trip? Now with the lunchtime traffic, she'll be stuck for ages. Her ringtone blares and she fights with the contents of her bag to pluck it out before it rings out.

"Jeff, hon."

"Hiya, gorgeous. Look, you aren't busy are ya?"

"Well, I *am* on my way to a crime scene."

"Oh yeah, that little kiddie?"

"How did you hear it was a kid?"

"It's all over the news."

Roberta extends her phone further enough away from her face so he doesn't hear her curse. Claire! That bitch from the national press. How did she find out something that Roberta hadn't? She wasn't even there.

"Christ, looks like I have more to do than I thought. Sorry babe, but I've got to go-"

"No, wait, Robby. There's someone here looking for you."

Roberta's breath catches in her throat.

CHAPTER 8:

Although the stairs seem to always smell, this apartment block is far better than the one Roberta had just moved out of. She was there for almost three years before she thought enough was enough. Student after student moving in either side of her and partying well into the night. But it was the only place that Roberta could afford. She had splashed out on a car when she'd gotten the reporter's job, knowing that if she had to rely on public transport around these parts, the story will have been and gone. Yesterday's news.

It was nowhere near as bad as her place on Promised Hill though. The one the council gave her after her parents chucked her out. It may have only been two streets away, but it felt like a million miles from living under their roof. Thankfully, she was only there until she could get a decent wage from the paper. Finding the flats in the student areas were fine. Renting was cheap and included all bills. But now, coming into her mid-20s, Roberta needed a quieter life. The hours at the office were hard enough, without not being able to sleep for the three or four spare hours she had before she'd have to be back there.

Jeff and Roberta had been dating for two years now, and when they got engaged, they found no reason why they shouldn't move in together. They found this quiet little number on the corner of town, and they were happy.

Roberta opens the door and peeks her head around.

"Robby!"

A chubby little blonde girl bounces through the living room, wrapping her arms around Roberta's legs.

"Hiya, Lyd. What are you doing here? Shouldn't you be in school?"

Lydia drops her head and runs back over to the sofa. Picking up the remote, she turns the volume on Nickelodeon back on.

"Lyd, what's happened?"

Lydia still averts her eyes. Turning off the TV by the switch, Roberta sits down and pulls Lydia into a hug.

"She just appeared this morning at the front door."

Jeff stands at the door to the kitchen, sipping his coffee in his navy dressing gown.

"Did you walk from school?"

Lydia nods sheepishly, digging her head into Roberta's leg.

"Oh, Lyd. That's dangerous. You could've been-"

"I waited for the green man every time," Lydia protests, sticking her arm in the air, fingers in a peace sign.

"Well look, you know that everyone has to go to school."

"But I don't wanna."

"I know. No one ever does. But look at me and Jeff now. All grown up with jobs and that. You need to go to school to learn things and be like us. Otherwise you'll end up like…"

Roberta coughs and glances over at Jeff, eyes wide in a silent '*help*.'

"Er… Or you'll have no job and no money. No house. You'll be out on the street begging for food like them people outside Ben's Palace," Jeff winks at Roberta, joining the duo on the sofa.

"Or like Mummy and Daddy," Lydia sulks.

Roberta and Jeff share a concerned glance. Lydia is only coming eight, but has already seen too much of the world living with Roberta's parents.

"Look, Lyd. Mummy and Daddy love you. Very much. But they…"

Roberta purses her lips and gazes out of the window. How can she begin to tell her sister that her mum and dad are using her to get money from the government to spend on booze, fags and drugs?

"They get angry at me."

Lydia looks up, tears in her eyes.

"Now why would they do that?"

"I dropped a plate last night. By accident. They got me a Happy Meal for dinner and I was putting the chicken nuggets on a plate with my ketchup, but the plate slipped and smashed. I cut my foot."

"You did? Oh, Lyd. Let me see."

Roberta helps Lydia off with her plimsolls and pulls her school tights down. That's when Roberta sees the bruises and cuts on Lydia's legs. Is that a cigarette burn? Jeff coughs and stands, retreating to the kitchen.

"Lydia... How did you get these marks?"

Lydia grabs a pillow from beside her and covers her legs, shaking her head.

"It's only a tiny cut, look."

She brandishes her foot in front of Roberta's face, but Roberta takes back her pillow.

"Did Mummy or Daddy do this to you?"

Lydia looks away, fresh tears in her eyes. Jeff returns with a thick plaster to tie around her foot.

"There. Good as new?"

"Good as new," Lydia smiles and gives Jeff a hug.

"Look, Lyd. You're going to have to go to school. I have to go to work and-"

"But Jeff's here. Can't I stay tonight? Oh, please, Robby. Please?"

Roberta exhales and glances up at Jeff. He shrugs his shoulders in surrender. She reverts her eyes to Lydia, on her knees on the floor, her hands clasped together like she's praying, her huge eyes gazing up at her.

"Fine, but only for tonight, you hear me? We'll take you to school first thing tomorrow."

Lydia jumps up and celebrates, hugging the couple.

"What do you say we go to the McDonald's down the road, shall we? Get you an eight pack of nuggets," Jeff slaps his hands off his bare knees, before standing up.

Her eyes widen, giving them an even bigger look.

"Eight? That will do me breakfast, lunch *and* dinner!"

CHAPTER 9:

"He's still not back from the morgue."

Dawson and Simpson have joined Donna back in her house.

"He left over an hour ago. Have you tried contacting him?" Simpson cocks her head to the side.

"No. He doesn't like me calling him when he's out," Donna fusses over the pillow on the armchair again. Dawson watches as she stares at it plump back to life, like lungs breathing in, after her flattening it.

"Where would he be, Donna?"

Donna glares at him with wild eyes.

"I couldn't say. He wouldn't like me tellin'."

Simpson steps in front of Dawson, hands around her belt.

"Donna, we need to-"

"Mummy, who's these people?"

The detectives turn to see a young brown-haired girl lingering in the doorway, the local primary school uniform hanging limply from her thin frame.

"These are the police, Clara."

Clara steps timidly into the room and hides behind her mother, peaking her head around to stare fascinatedly at the detectives. The family liaison officer crosses the threshold towards them, extending his hand for Donna to shake. Clara's tattered school bag hanging from his shoulder, making the scene almost comical.

"Hi, Donna. My name's Nick. I'm here t-"

"Why did you bring her home from school?"

Nick looks taken aback.

"Our orders," Simpson gazes at Donna suspiciously.

"I didn't want her to have any part of it," Donna escorts Clara through to the kitchen and closes the door with a short snap.

"On the contrary, Donna, I feel like she should be involved."

"She's too young."

"That may be the case, but she still has to be interviewed and-"

"No. I don't want my daughter being brought into this. She'll have nightmares. She's too-"

"Are you helping find Jilly?"

Donna's head snaps to the kitchen door, lying ajar as Clara stands on tip toes, still pushing the handle down, biting a finger on her other hand.

"Clara, don-"

"Yes, honey. We are. Is she missing?"

Simpson ignores Donna's silent protests and crosses the tiny living room and slips down on to her haunches to come level with the girl.

"She wasn't in her room this morning. I went in to say good morning and she was gone."

"Is that right? Where would she have gone, Clara?"

Clara innocently shrugs her shoulders and extends her arms dramatically.

"Most of the time when I want her she's in her room doing her homework. She does hard spelling tests."

"But what about the times she isn't there, where is she?"

Clara sticks out her bottom lips and hums in thought.

"She likes to play with Bobby."

"Bobby who, darling?"

"I don't know. He has yellow hair."

Simpson smiles as she stands and glances around at Dawson.

"We need to find your daddy, do you know where he is?" Dawson smiles at the youngster, who can't be more than seven-years-old.

"He works on Mondays. He always comes back with fish and chips when he works," Clara giggles.

Dawson and Simpson excuse themselves and huddle in the narrow hallway, their faces illuminated by the misty light protruding through the distorted window on the front door.

"We have to find him, we need a statement from this family."

"I know, Simpson. But where can we start?"

"Have you seen the empty cans littered across the floor? I say the pubs. Put a call around for all pubs to be checked on Promised Hill, starting with those in close proximity to David's Lane."

CHAPTER 10:

Dylan's smile is wiped from his face when Dawson barges into the house. Closing the door, he joins the detective and Mandy in the living room.

"Just a few questions for you two," Dawson sniffs as he makes himself comfortable.

"Would you like a cup of tea, detective?" Mandy smiles.

"No, I plan on not staying longer than I have to."

Mandy and Dylan share concerned glances after noticing Dawson's upturned nose, before sitting on the settee opposite him.

"So, how long have you known Jill Yates?"

"Pfft," Dylan and his wife share another look. "Two… Maybe three years?"

"And you say she was friends with your son, Bobby?"

"Yeah, they're good mates. Met at school. Think they sat beside each other in Art class."

"Could there be a romantic connection?"

The couple stare at the detective perplexed.

"He's 15, sir."

"Never too young to develop hormones, Mr Gardener. Don't you remember your teenage years?"

"Try to forget them," Dylan chuckles nervously.

"Well I'm sure by the time you were 15 that you were interested in girls, were you not?"

Dylan fidgets uncomfortably.

"Well... I suppose, yeah. But nothing ever came of it. Don't think I had a girlfriend until I was 17 at the most."

Dawson glares at the man with his teeth clenched. He seems comfortable enough with his wife, his hand resting on her knee. Most kids around these parts are pregnant and high school drop outs by the time they're 16. Is he lying to Dawson? Pretending he didn't have a girlfriend until he was nearly an adult?

"Nevertheless, your son could well be interested in girls now, surely?"

"I can't bear the thought," Mandy chuckles. "You see all sorts around this place. We feel like we've brought him up right. Not always easy when he sees kids his age sniffing glue when we're just taking a trip to the shops."

Dawson nods, he doesn't need to be convinced of the state of Promised Hill.

"So, he's never mentioned any romantic connections with Jill Yates?"

"Not that we know of. Like we said, we think they were only friends," Mandy blinks. "Sorry, but what has this got to do with her murder?" she says, eyeballing his notepad.

"We just have to approach this investigation from every angle," Dawson gives her his best fake smile. "Anyway, were you aware of any boyfriend in the girl's life?"

Dylan's head turns towards his wife, who protrudes her lip, glances up at the ceiling and shakes her head slightly.

"No. Our Bobby didn't mention anything, and I never heard anything from Jill herself. She was a very quiet girl."

"Care to explain?"

"Well... She would stay for dinner sometimes and you would sort of have to force conversation out of her, you know? Not a big talker. Bobby said she was just shy."

"Did she seem happy?"

"She didn't seem unhappy. She wasn't depressed, if that's what you're thinking?"

"And how do you know that?"

"She just wasn't. No signals. Bobby would've told us."

"What has he told you about her?"

Mandy exhales and looks at her husband for reassurance.

"Not an awful lot actually," Dylan takes the wheel again. "Erm... She loved English. Always asked for extra books to take home. Bobby thought that was strange, but he hates reading. Very sporty, kept winning the gold medals on sports days. Apart from that, nothing springs to mind. Nothing of use to explain why she ended up in our back alley."

Dawson nods and glances between the couple, who fidget uncomfortably.

"Fine. Do you mind if I come back later to interview your son?"

"No, not at all," Mandy smiles as the party of three stand. "Detective..." she leans forward sheepishly, "should we be worried? For Bobby?"

"We don't know yet, Mrs Gardener. It is too early to tell...."

CHAPTER 11:

Cherrie Cooke hobbles back to her armchair, her knuckles white around her walking stick. Falling back into her original position before she was interrupted, she exhales dramatically.

"Gettin' old," she smiles at Simpson.

Simpson beams back, placing herself delicately on the edge of the two-piece sofa beside the elderly woman. Cherrie reaches for her twenty-pack of cigarettes, before extending the lighter to the DS. Simpson shakes her head timidly, waiting for Cherrie to inhale her first fix before starting questioning.

"I'm not sure if you've heard what's been going on this morning, Miss Cooke. But Rong Valley's Police Department have just launched a murder investigation. We'd just like to ask you a few questions, if you don't mind."

Cherrie nods her head as she takes another drag, only slightly distracting herself away from the TV.

"Okay, so how long have you been living in this house?"

Cherrie shrugs.

"As long as I can remember. It was my mother's house, and she left it to me."

"So you've lived here all your life?"

Cherrie nods again.

"And how is your relationship with the neighbours?"

Cherrie considers this question, taking a few mouthfuls of nicotine before giving her answer through the exhale.

"People around here keep themselves to themselves."

"So you don't know the Yates' next door?"

"I would know of them. Say hello to them if I passed them on the street. But I'd never ask them in for Sunday tea."

"Do you have access to the alleyway behind your house, linking this row of houses to the rows on Windsor Place?"

"I'm sure I do. My nephew usually comes to take the bins out, so he would know where the key is."

"Your nephew?"

"Yeah, what of him?"

"Who is he?"

"Darren Ward. My sister Annie's kid. What does him taking out my bins every week got to do

49

with the Yates' next door? And this so-called murder investigation?"

"Miss Cooke, a girl's body was found in that alley this morning. We have since got confirmation that the body belongs to your next-door neighbour, Jill Yates."

The old lady's face doesn't so much as flinch.

"Is that the older one or the youngster?"

"She is 15-years-old, so the eldest."

Cherrie nods and lights another cigarette.

"Shame, innit?"

"Sorry?"

"Just such a young life wasted."

"Yes, Miss Cooke. It's awful. I'm here to ask whether you heard or seen anything out of the ordinary? Perhaps in the early hours of the morning or late last night?"

Simpson waits with bated breath as Cherrie takes another drag.

"No, sorry. Was in bed after Heartbeat. Slept like a baby."

Simpson can't hide her disappointment as she gazes out onto the street. She chews her lip for a few minutes as she waits for Cherrie to finish her third cigarette. When she stubs it out, she reaches for the pack again. Simpson lunges forward and beats her to it, the two women's hands brushing.

"What the-"

"Please, Cherrie," Simpson begs, holding the cigarettes at arm's length away from the old lady, who leans off her chair as far as she can without falling off, trying to snap them back. "Can you tell me everything you know about the Yates family? They've lived here long enough for you to have an opinion on them. We need to get to the bottom of this."

"And what? You're just going to withhold my fags until I spill?"

"Spill what?"

Cherrie recoils in her chair and purses her lips.

"They're just not my type of people, alright?"

"And why's that?"

"Always fighting and going on. Dad's a drunk. Mum's definitely on something. Poor kiddies have had a shitty life. The eldest was different though. Seemed like she was going somewhere. Always reading or studying. She could've got her ass out of here. That's all I know about her. Just through snatches of seeing her over the years. I don't know what's been going on or what could've happened her. Just find out soon before any more kiddies get hurt. Now give me back my fags!"

CHAPTER 12:

Kane is slumped over the bar in The Rusty Crown when Dawson joins him on the stools. He gives the detective a squinty eyed look before slamming his hands on the counter top.

"Another, Kenny."

The barman, Kenny, sloshes another whiskey into Kane's outstretched hand, who nods his thanks and swigs it back.

"You – want anything?" he hiccups.

"No thank you, Kane. We've been looking everywhere for you."

"I – I saw the copper in uniform in earlier," he sways on the stool, flicking his hand backwards towards the door. "Lucky he didn't get a crack on the head, some of the yobs around this place."

Dawson nods and glances around at the dingy pub. Spare of a dart board and a battered TV, there was nothing else of worth or interest. Looks like the kind of place he'd shut down for selling drugs over the counter. But he's not here for that now.

"C'mon, Kane. Let's get you home, shall we?"

"Are you havin' a laugh, sir?"

Simpson stands in the Yates' front yard, mouth open.

"He's pissed. Threw up all down his front on the car journey home. He'll be of no use until later. We can still speak to Donna and the girl now."

"You *do* know that in most cases of murdered children it is almost always the parents responsible-"

"Sshh," Dawson waves his hands and leads Simpson out onto the pavement. "We need these guys on our side. This is Rong Valley, Simpson. Nothing of that sort happens here. Regardless, he *will* be interviewed and alibis checked. But not just yet. He's making no sense. Anyway, how did you get on with the neighbours?"

"Well, number 50 is abandoned," she points behind her. "I rang the landlord and it's been getting refurbished for a few months now. Hasn't been lived in in almost two years. Number 54 is an elderly lady called Cherrie Cooke. She can barely walk. Has her nephew, Darren Ward, come and help her about the house once in a while. And get this, he takes her bins out for her."

"Potential suspect?"

"Can't hurt to enquire into it."

"Good job, Simpson. Can I trust you to follow that up?"

"Already underway, sir."

"Great. Now... How should we approach this?" he turns towards the house and stares in the living room window at the drawn curtains. "Donna is very on edge. Who do you think she trusts more?"

"I'll question her. As long as you can pretend to be human long enough to get some information out of the girl. Clara, isn't it?"

Dawson nods his head and resists a smirk.

"I think you're forgetting that I *do* have three girls of my own, Sergeant."

"I wouldn't expect anything less, sir."

"Now, let's get this started before I have to pick my youngest up from school."

CHAPTER 13:

"She was in bed by 10pm. She is every night," Donna's eyes shift towards Kane, sitting casually in the armchair, only he's asleep with his jeans at his ankles.

"And you don't remember her leaving the house or acting suspicious?" Simpson nods.

"No. She's a good girl."

"When was the last time you saw her?"

"Dinner time."

"Which was?"

"After six."

"What did you eat?"

"Sausages and mash."

"Where was Kane?"

Donna fidgets uncomfortably, her lip trembling.

"It's okay. He's out for the count. We'll be asking him anyway."

"He was at the pub."

"Which pub?"

"The Rusty Crown."

"Does he go there a lot?"

"No more so than any other man," Donna chuckles slightly.

"When did he come home?"

"About 11ish."

"And then what happened?"

"He sat and watched TV. I made him chicken and chips and then went to bed."

"And did he follow you? Or did he..."

Simpson cocks her head towards the living room behind her.

"No, he made it to bed."

"How long after you?"

"10... Maybe 15 minutes later."

Simpson eyes Donna suspiciously. She can't help but feel like Donna's hiding something.

"Detective Dawson has been up there a long time with Clara," Donna gazes at the roof, like she can see what's happening.

"I'm sure he won't be much longer. Can I ask you a few more questions please?"

Donna shivers and returns to her mug of tea.

"Did Jill ever confide in you? About bullies or anything strange?"

"No. Her life was very boring."

"Do you know Darren Ward?"

Donna sticks out her lip as she shakes her head. "The name doesn't ring a bell. Should it?"

Simpson ignores the question.

"Any boyfriends or fights with friends? Anything out of the ordinary?"

"No. Like I said, Jill was very normal. Very boring."

The creaks of the old house indicate that Dawson is descending the stairs, and Donna shoves the half-full mug of tea in the sink before quickly scurrying out towards him. Holding Clara's hand, she leads her back into the kitchen. Nick looks between Dawson and Simpson and digests their disappointed faces.

"Sorry, Simpson. But I have to go collect Kyra. Helen's in Birmingham for the day. I'll leave her off at my mum's and meet you back at the station."

Simpson nods her head with pursed lips, gazing around the room and thinking of what to do next.

Dawson closes the metal gate of number 52 and makes a run for his car, hypervigilant of his surroundings and whether there are any hidden members of the media. But as he's turning out of Connolly's Estate, he almost forgets to brake as he's too busy staring at the other side of the road.

"Alicia," he shouts as he rolls down his window.

She flicks her hair back to see the source of the call, and her face drops. There she is, still in her school uniform, hand-in-hand with a boy a few feet taller. Dawson's blood boils as he stares at his white PVC jacket and black tracksuit bottoms, with his black Nike cap covering most of his face.

"Dad," Alicia exhales, making the mystery lad scurry off down the street and jump a low wall into a neighbouring estate. By the time Dawson has exited his vehicle and crossed the road, he's nowhere to be seen.

CHAPTER 14:

Roberta nestles down onto the Gardener's sofa, the mug of tea gratefully received. The couple sit either side of their son, Bobby, who had been called home from school due to the ordeal. His huge dimples are prominent on his otherwise soft face. The kid doesn't look his age. If Roberta passed him on the street she would mistake him for a primary school student. He fidgets uncomfortably as his mum tries to play with his hair, which has enough gel on it to do Jeff a month or two. She noticed the smell of his cologne on his school uniform as soon as he walked in too.

"So, Bobby. My name's Roberta Holmes. I'm the crime editor for the Herald. As I'm sure your parents have already told you, the body of your friend, Jill, was found in the alley behind your house this morning. I'm here to celebrate her life. I don't want her to become just another statistic, and people like you are going to help me prevent that from happening. I know you're upset, we all are. But if you could, please, tell us a bit about Jill."

Bobby's jaw is clenched, trying desperately to hold back tears. His mother notices and pulls him in for a hug, which he momentarily resists, before letting himself give way to the grief. Roberta watches as he shrinks down a few sizes as the tension and the tears erupt all over his mother's blouse.

"Were you good friends?"

He nods and sniffs. "She was really sweet. Always up for a laugh and was nice to everyone... Despite where she came from."

Roberta's eyes narrow as Mandy Gardener nudges her son aggressively.

"Care to explain?"

Bobby shuffles his clumpy school shoes on the carpet uncomfortably.

"Her dad's a dick."

"Bobby!"

"What? He is. I've only been around there a handful of times and he's always giving us dirty looks and pissed off his head."

"Alright, Bobby. I know you're angry and upset, but we didn't bring you up to speak about people like that. Especially to a reporter."

Roberta smiles innocently at Mandy.

"Don't worry, I've been around to the Yates' already and seen for myself that Jill's dad was asleep on the sofa, clearly too far gone with drink. Her mum wasn't very cooperative either. Wouldn't speak to me. The FLO also wasn't too happy."

The family of three give the reporter a confused look.

"Oh, sorry. The FLO. The family liaison officer. I'm going to try again tomorrow once they've had a day to digest what has happened. In the meantime-"

Roberta is interrupted by the doorbell echoing through the hall. Mandy apologises, excusing herself, and shuffles off to answer the door. Seconds later, DS Simpson trudges into the room and gives Roberta a look of disgust.

"Have you no shame?"

"Excuse me?"

"We haven't even finished our interviews yet and you're already snooping your nose in."

"I apologise, Sergeant, but however this looks, I assure-"

"Get out now, I wish to speak to the boy."

Roberta's mouth falls open. She glances at the Gardeners, who look anywhere else but at the journalist. Their own house being taken over by a tyrant like Simpson, Roberta thinks, disgusted.

She coughs awkwardly before standing, retrieving her card from her bag.

"If there's anything else you'd like to talk about, Bobby. Please don't hesitate to ask."

Bobby takes the card with another sniff, before thanking her. As Roberta steps over the threshold into the hall, she turns to say her goodbyes, but is met with Simpson snapping the living room door shut mere inches from her nose.

CHAPTER 15:

Bobby seems a lot more reserved now that he is in the company of the detective.

"You were good friends with Jill, yeah?"

He nods politely, but still won't give her a second glance.

"Well that's good. You know why? You can give us an insight into her life. Where did she hang out? Who were her other friends? Did she confide in you? No pebble is too small to be left unturned, Bobby. And you can be a massive part of this investigation. Murder doesn't happen in Rong Valley. I'm sure we all know that. And you know why? Because we're a close-knit community. We respect one another, including ourselves in the police force. Therefore, we need to bring the Yates, and you in a way, justice. And I promise you, I will not rest until we do that. So, first thing's first, can you think of *anyone* who would want to cause Jill any harm?"

For the first time Bobby glares into Simpson's eyes, before sniffing and leaning forward.

"Jill was a lovely person. No one would wish that on her. She was my best friend. And I'm not gonna have the likes of you coming in here and saying she had enemies, because she didn't."

And with that, he leans back and crosses his arms, a snarl outlining his once soft features.

"Robert Leon Gardener!"

Mandy looks horrified.

"It's okay, Mrs Gardener. I understand this is a horrible time for young Bobby here. It's a horrible time for everyone. But I can assure you, Bobby, that we are not here to pick at the wound. We just want to get the person responsible behind bars. We don't want what happened late last night or in the early hours of this morning repeated. I don't want anyone else getting hurt, somehow I'm sure that you agree with me. Yeah?"

Bobby purses his lips and glances at the wall before nodding slightly.

"So, Bobby. Everything that you say is going to help us. Please…"

A few moments of silence follow, before Bobby wipes a single tear from his eye.

"I think you need to speak to Scott Woodhouse."

Simpson reaches for her notepad, visibly shocked that he has offered information so soon.

"I'm sorry, Bobby. Who?"

"Scott Woodhouse."

Her pen hovers over the pad, waiting patiently to extort its ink in the form of a lead.

"I'm sorry, but can you elaborate?"

"She's been hanging out with him the past few weeks. I don't know a lot about him, just that he was very interested in her."

"And her with him?"

Bobby shrugs and looks out of the window.

"Bobby... Were they in a relationship?"

"She wouldn't talk to me about him. All I found out was his name. I wasn't happy wi-"

His eyes widen as he cuts himself off and looks down at his lap, his fingers trembling.

"You weren't happy about what, Bobby?"

"I didn't want him seeing her."

"And why is that, Bobby? Were you jealous?"

Bobby's head snaps back up and he resumes to glare at the detective.

"No! Jesus. That's all everyone ever says. Can't a boy and a girl just be friends without everyone going on like they're boyfriend and girlfriend? We're just friends. We *were* just friends..."

His lip trembles and tears spring to his eyes once more.

"Okay, I'm sorry, Bobby. But we do have to cover every aspect of this investigation. So, Jill was seeing this Scott Woodhouse?"

He nods again.

"And you weren't happy?"

He shakes his head.

"So, why weren't you happy."

Bobby bites his lip and looks the detective straight in the eye.

"'cause he's older. *Much* older."

CHAPTER 16:

"What the hell were you thinking?"

Dawson has marched his daughter to the car and is speeding in the direction of Kyra's school, skimming cars as he overtakes them, ignoring their blaring horns and their owner's rude gestures.

"I'm old enough to have a boyfriend, Dad!"

"You bloody are not. And what? Think if you are that you can waltz around Promised Hill of all places? And when you're supposed to be at school? Well I oughta," Dawson's fingers clench on the steering wheel, making the leather burn into his palms. "I've just been at the house of a family who have had their 15-year-old girl murdered, Alicia. *Murdered*. In Promised Hill. And there's you running those same streets with a strange man. And did you see the state of him? He probably had a knife in his pocket. Ready to get you home and do God only knows what to you. You are *not* to see that boy again. You're under house arrest. Only allowed to leave to go to school and piano practice, you hear me?"

68

"I'm not one of your fucking suspects, Dad," Alicia squeals, kicking the glove compartment and shielding her face, stubbornly hiding the oncoming tears from her father. "You can't control me. Carl is lovely. We've been seeing each other for three weeks and you knew nothing about it. I never told you because I knew you would react like this. You did the same thing when Sue said she was going to the cinema with that lad Tom all those years ago. Mum thought you were going to pick her up in a bloody police car. I hate you!"

Her attempts to hide her sobs are shattered when they break through into her speech on the last three syllables. As Dawson reaches a red light that he's too slow to slide through, he brings the car to an emergency stop. They both sit in silence for several minutes, before Dawson pushes the car into first gear and turns right onto Rod's Lane, adjacent to Kyra's school. When the car is parked in the visitor's car park, Dawson turns to his daughter and watches as she hastily reapplies her make up.

"Why didn't you tell me?"

Alicia turns to him, one side of her face still a mess of running mascara and extends her hands in confusion.

"Why the hell would I?"

"Does your mother know?"

She shifts uncomfortably in her seat, returning her attention to the wing mirror.

"Why didn't you tell me, Alicia?"

"Because of where he's from," she spits at him. "You think everyone is the same in Promised Hill. Drug dealers, smack heads, fraudsters. You talk about it all the time. But what you don't see are there *are* genuine people that live there, okay? People that don't have much money. People that can't get jobs. People that are sick or disabled. They can't just decide to live in a lovely house like ours. So they have no choice."

"And this... Carl is one of them?"

She shrugs.

"He still lives with his mum and dad. His dad works in a factory in the city for buttons and his mum hasn't worked since she had him and his brothers. Couldn't afford childcare."

They see Kyra skip out of one of the cabin classrooms, pointing towards the car as the teaching assistant waves her off. Dawson raises a finger in affirmation and pulls his seatbelt on.

"So this is serious? Between you and Carl?"

Alicia nods, still glaring out of the window.

"Then ask him over. Maybe Thursday night? If he'll like your mother's stew."

Alicia shoots her father an alarming look, before Kyra gracelessly yanks the door to the backseat open and topples unceremoniously inside.

"Hi Daddy. Alicia what are you doing here?"

Dawson and Alicia share a look.

"Erm... I picked Alicia up from school already, Ky. She was feeling ill. So you be a good girl and let her watch her shows when we get home and you can bring her soup."

"I will. I'm sorry you feel sick, Leesh. We can watch Friends and I won't complain about not getting to see my programmes."

Dawson chuckles as he drives out of the school and homeward bound, but not before glancing at Alicia gazing out of the window. Still sulking, but he can see a glimmer of hope behind his little girl's eyes.

CHAPTER 17:

"So, let me get this straight."

Dawson has gathered everyone in the incident room upon hearing new conclusions from DS Simpson. On the centre of the huge board in the corner is a school picture of Jill Yates, looking innocent with her shy smile. Right beside is the picture forensics had taken just this morning. A few years have passed between the photographs, but aging is not the only difference. Dawson now sees what Dylan Gardener meant when he said that it took a while to recognise her. The blows to her face were significantly masking the pretty girl underneath, with the blue and yellowing bruises concealing her soft features.

Arrows lead out from the two images, dispersing off to other pictures. One photo is of Darren Ward, a police custody snap taken a few years back when he was arrested for a drunken scrap in the town centre. Another holds a black outline of a head and shoulders with a question mark over the face, a sloppy substitute in the absence of a genuine photo. The name underneath states that this indicates Scott Woodhouse. But now, Simpson has placed Bobby Gardener's school photo at the end of another arrow.

"You think that Bobby could be a suspect?"

"Yes, sir."

"Forgive me, but I don't see how."

"I think he has feelings for Jill. Or at least *had* feelings towards her. He got very defensive when I questioned him about their relationship. Also, as we now know, there seemed to be another boy that came onto the scene."

She waves her pen over the shadow image representing Scott.

"Bobby doesn't talk about Scott kindly. Said he's far older than Jill and he wasn't happy about it. Maybe jealousy took a rude form in him. After all, he does have a key to the back gate out into the alley."

"Okay, I trust you've put operations in place to chase the relationship up?"

"I have officers on the ground patrolling the school. They'll be speaking to school friends, relatives, teachers. And we're currently trying to zone in on the whereabouts of Scott."

"Great. Good work, Simpson. And Darren?"

"He lives just off Rong Valley Park. I was just going to go pay him a visit. Apart from his initial arrest, his record is clean. Works for his uncle's butchers. But he, also, has access to the alley through his aunt Cherrie Cooke's house."

"But so does everyone on the joining streets, surely?"

"True, sir. And that's why I've got more uniforms combing through the homes, interviewing the inhabitants."

"Always one step ahead, aren't you Simpson?"

"Thank you, sir."

"Right, so everyone has been briefed and knows what needs to be done?"

Dawson pushes out his chest and turns towards the few dozen beady eyes surrounding the long desk. A few nod their heads as they begin to chatter amongst themselves.

"Wait."

The team, and Dawson, turn towards Simpson, who hasn't moved from her stance beside the board.

"I want to throw one more name in the midst."

And with that, she clears her throat and picks up another picture. She leans heavily on it for the tac to stick to the board, before stepping back to reveal Kane Yates' face. Whispers flare up in the room again, with a few adding a shocked intake of breath. Dawson marches straight over.

"What the *hell* are you doing, Simpson?" he hisses in her ear.

"Kane Yates has yet to be questioned," Simpson ignores her superior and continues to address the room as a whole. "Through forensic research and findings in the post mortem, we believe that Jill's murderer is healthy and fit. She received blow after blow and was both kicked and punched repeatedly. Because we do not have a statement from her father, or any other indication that he is innocent, he *is* still a suspect. I will proceed to interview him now, if you'd care to join me Inspector?"

She smiles sweetly at Dawson, who turns his nose up at her. When the team notice the awkward air in the room and start to slip out, he leans his head in towards hers once again.

"Are you trying to make a fool out of me?" he whispers.

"No, sir. On the contrary, the opposite. I want to find the perpetrator-"

"And you're saying I don't?"

"I never said that, sir. But I believe you're blinded by your passion due to your family relations with the deceased. You've refused to conduct compulsory duties in this investigation. I have half a mind to inform the Superintend-"

"No, Simpson. There is no need. Maybe I have been a little careless, but I assure you that the last time I came within spitting distance of the Yates' was all those decades ago. However, I hold a responsibility to them, not only as a relative, but as the Detective Inspector of Rong Valley's Police Department. You're right, we need to eliminate him from our enquiries. He should be awake by now, if he hasn't already went back on the drink."

CHAPTER 18:

"You better shut your fucking mouth, you hear me?"

Kane is towering over Donna. She's cowering between two cupboards in the corner of the kitchen, sobbing uncontrollably. On the floor lie discarded, half cooked peas and sweetcorn, dispersed around the room when Kane lifted the saucepan from the stove. The base of the pan is still blistering hot, and it takes all of Kane's energy not to bring it down on Donna's pretty little fingers, shielding her head and face from him. The semi-boiled water from the pan soaks into Kane's polo shirt, but he doesn't so much as flinch.

"I didn't say anything. I promise, K."

"Well what did you say?"

"I told them that she was in bed. Last time I saw her was when I made her dinner. She went off to do homework."

"And what about me, you bitch? What did you say about me?"

"I didn't say anything."

77

"They wouldn't have taken that for an answer."

"I just said you were out."

"Out where?" he screams, brandishing the pan inches closer to Donna's head, her screams muffled by her blouse.

"I just said you were out. Went for a pint or two. When you came back they were both asleep and I made your tea. Then we both went to bed. That's all, K. You have to believe me."

Kane breathes heavily, his stomach swirling from the drink and sick from the smell of cabbage boiling beside him. He grunts and drops the pan, falling with a clatter next to his wife.

"Good. If I hear you've been saying anything different…"

He turns and pushes the door to the living room forcefully, before storming off to turn the shower on.

Kane hobbles down the stairs when he's satisfied that the remnants of this morning's day drinking have been successfully washed down the drain. He reaches the final few steps and halts. From here, he can hear voices in the living room. Familiar voices. He throws open the door to see both DI Dawson and DS Simpson sitting on his settee.

"Kane."

Dawson stands and outstretches his hand.

"Detective," he says, shaking it.

"Please, call me Donald."

Kane smiles and turns towards his wife. Her lip trembles discreetly as she vacates his seat, before migrating to the kitchen. The trio take their seats.

"So, Kane. Sorry to barge in like this again, but I'm sure you know that we have to take statements t-"

"I fully understand. Do whatever you need to do."

Dawson smiles at Kane sympathetically.

"As I'm sure you can guess, you were a bit worse for wear earlier and unfit for interview."

"You could say that," Kane chuckles, before burying his head in his hands dramatically. "I just didn't know what way to cope. When I saw her lying there... The whole time on the way over... I – I – I just hoped and hoped that it wasn't her. Then when I saw her... Something just popped. Like I wasn't thinking straight. I left the station and wandered aimlessly through the streets. Somehow, I ended up in The Rusty Crown. It's my local. I needed a bit of company. Some people who didn't know, obviously. I wanted to pretend it wasn't happening. That it was all a dream. I drank to numb the pain. Too much, clearly."

Kane looks up at the detectives and gives a small smile.

"I know these are not reasonable enough excuses for my behaviour, but I sincerely am sorry. And please tell Nick that I'm sorry too. When I saw him in here, I just wanted him to leave. Didn't want attention or extra support. Wanted to pretend everything was normal."

"We will let him know," Dawson nods his head.

"I've probably set yourselves back, and through that have messed up the start of this investigation. Of course I want you to find the bastard who did this to my daughter. Please, ask away. I'll tell you what I know."

CHAPTER 19:

Roberta battles with the lock into her flat, shoving her entire weight on the door, but it still won't budge. She turns the key again, but it's met with a blockade. It can't turn any further. Surely she hasn't broken it already? Almost instantly, the lock clicks and out steps Jeff.

"Sorry, hon. Lydia wouldn't settle unless she was sure that the door was definitely locked. I showed her that no one could get in if I had my key pressed in."

He showcases his key and flashes her a soft smile, before pecking her on the cheek.

"How was your day?"

"Stressful. The police are giving us peanuts. Luckily I've got some decent information that will be run in the morning."

"Care to explain?"

Roberta raises an eyebrow and widens her eyes in a silent '*ssh*' as they cross the threshold into the kitchen, before cocking her head at Lydia, who sits at the table with a plate of turkey dinosaurs and spaghetti hoops, carelessly kicking her legs back and forth below the table.

"Hi, Robby."

"Hiya, Lyd. What did you two get up to today?"

"Oh, it was good fun. First Jeff took me to McDonald's and then we went a walk in the park. It was kinda cold, but Jeff put his coat over me. It ran along the floor and I thought it was funny. I looked silly," she giggles, before beheading a t-rex with her teeth.

"Sounds like you two had a great day," Roberta smiles, flopping herself down in the chair beside her. "I brought back a new pair of socks and knickers from the shops and some princess pyjamas for you to sleep in tonight. Jeff's working very early tomorrow, so I'll take you into school in the morning. And you *have* to stay there, you hear me? Only bad girls don't go to school."

"Am I bad?"

"You were today," Roberta scolds, before delving her hands beneath Lydia's armpits, forcing her to burst into a fit of giggles. "But now that you know it's bad you won't do it again, right?"

Lydia's laughter ceases and she looks at the floor noddingly.

"Good girl, now eat up and then we'll get you a bath before bed."

CHAPTER 20:

"Alright, alright. Hold your horses."

Janine Holmes sticks her newly lit cigarette between her teeth and reaches for the front door, vibrating with the persistent knocks that have been going on for the better part of two minutes. The door, not to mention the bell, broke years ago, so she gives it the signature tug to fight it open. She's met with Roberta on her doorstep. Taking the cigarette from her mouth, she breathes the smoke outwards, momentarily obscuring her from view. But when it clears, she realises she isn't dreaming, or hallucinating from the last drug she'd taken. God knows what she is onto now. Roberta really is standing there.

"Jesus, Roberta. Long time, no speak."

"Pleasure, I'm sure."

Roberta moves forward to enter the house, but Janine presses her body between the frame and the door. She gives a sickly smile, showing her rotting teeth.

"What do you want?"

"Lovely way to greet your daughter, eh?"

"A daughter we haven't seen or heard of in months."

"And I wonder why?"

"Who is it?" Ian calls from the sofa.

"Your loving daughter," Janine calls back.

"Well tell her to hurry up and get in here. Stop bickering on the doorstep. We don't need someone else complaining to the social. They're around here often enough as it is."

Roberta skirts around her mother and trudges into the dingy living room. There sits her father, face down on the coffee table snorting some substance, the name Roberta can only guess. It looks different to what he took when she lived here.

"For fuck sake, Dad."

He looks up when his eyes have cleared from the initial hit.

"Roberta? What the hell are you doing here? I thought you were the other one?"

"'*The other one.*' Yeah, fantastic parenting, Dad. And if I *was* Lydia, you would still be snorting whatever that dodgy Mickey lad has given you, I presume?"

Ian shrugs before popping a blue pill from his pocket.

85

"It's a free country. My house. And don't call Mickey dodgy. He's been supplying me with Grade A shit since before you were born."

"Charming. Look, I'm here to tell you that Lydia didn't go to school today. She landed at my front door. What happened last night?"

Janine joins Ian on the sofa as they pick through the contents of his jeans pocket. Every now and then, they see a pill and have a mini finger battle over who will get to consume it. When her father's pocket is presenting nothing but balls of cotton, her mother turns towards her.

"No clue what you're talking about."

"Don't play dumb with me. I've saw her arms and legs. And in the bath tonight I saw everything else. Every bruise and cut and burn. What the fuck have you been doing with her?"

The couple look at each other, almost as if they're bored, before returning their attention half-heartedly to their eldest daughter.

"If you're not careful, I'll get social services and even the police at your door in a heartbeat. They'll take Lydia into care and you can wave goodbye to your child support."

Now it looks like they're paying attention.

"Look, Lydia. There's n-"

"Roberta!"

"Oh for f... Roberta, then. There's no need to be so hasty," her father whines. "You won't know what it's like until you have rugrats of your own. They're dirty little shits. Get up to all sorts. We have done nothing to Lydia that we didn't do to you all those years ago. Looking back now, I'm sure you know that you deserved half of what you got-"

"Do not try and justify your torrents of abuse," Roberta screams. "I did *not* deserve to be locked in that suitcase."

"You were always a mouthy little shit. Can't remember what you did, but I'm sure it put the fear of God into you," her mother takes another drag of her cigarette.

"I was five-years-old!"

"Good enough for you," her dad spits.

"Look, this isn't about me. This is about Lydia. She's staying with me tonight. But she'll be back tomorrow. I don't get a lot of time off work, so I can't look after her. So, she'll be straight back here after school tomorrow. And I want you two ready. Clean this shithole up, get sober and act like fucking parents for once in your lives. Otherwise, she'll be taken from you, and your little income from her will be nowhere to be found. You hear me?"

BRADD CHAMBERS

Roberta gives her parents one last disgusted look and marches out of the house. Slamming the car door shut, she revs the engine and drives around the corner before coming to a stop and bursting into tears.

CHAPTER 21:

Dawson eases the door of Kyra's room closed, leaving a tiny gap for the hall light to protrude in. Scaring the monsters away, for Kyra at least. Dawson's monster is still on the loose. Through the gap, he sees his youngest daughter turn her back on him and sigh, letting sleep overpower her tiny mind. He smiles and tiptoes down the hall, coming to a rest outside Alicia's room.

She has been quiet all night. Despite being allowed to take the rest of the day off, she didn't so much as thank him when he brought her a blanket. In fact, she barely moved from the sofa at all. When dinner was ready, she sat and toyed with her steak before asking to be excused when the rest of them had finished. She hasn't vacated her room since. He taps lightly on the door before twisting the handle. There she lays on her stomach. 'To Kill A Mockingbird' perched lazily by her side, but the mobile phone in her hand taking priority over her studies.

"Mind if I come in a sec?"

Alicia shrugs as she takes her earphones out. Dawson perches himself idly on the end of her bed.

"Don't judge a man until you've walked a mile in his shoes."

Alicia looks at him confused. He reaches for her book.

"'To Kill A Mockingbird,' ain't it?"

"Erm... No. That's the concept I suppose, but not the correct quote."

"Aw, it's been thirty odd years since I read it. I'm good enough to remember that. A good concept to live your life by, though... Something I forget working in my job."

Alicia's muddled expression doesn't slide.

"Dad, is this your way of apologising for earlier?"

"Why should I apologise?"

"For scaring Carl away."

Dawson considers this before sighing and nodding his head.

"I suppose you could say that. I judged the fella just based on where he lived and what he was wearing. But you have no idea the things I see on that hill, Leesh. It would make your skin crawl."

"So you haven't seen anything like that anywhere else? Just Promised Hill?"

"I didn't say that. You get all sorts everywhere. But you can *always* bet that something shifty is going on around those parts. And I'd just left the home of a murdered girl. It put my mind on edge. I wasn't thinking straight. I'm sorry."

Alicia smiles and nods.

"You're forgiven, Dad. Now, if you don't mind, studying to do, essays to write. You know?"

"Of course, of course."

Dawson stands and starts towards the door, before swivelling around.

"That is, of course, if you don't want help with my fountain of Atticus Filch quotes and knowledge."

Alicia chuckles.

"Atticus *Finch*, Dad. Argus Filch is the caretaker from Harry Potter. Somehow, I think I'll manage."

Dawson returns the laugh and stares at his daughter a while longer.

"Dad, what's wrong?"

"Nothin'. Nothin'. It's just…"

He sighs.

"You wouldn't happen to know Jill Yates, would you?"

Alicia sticks out her lip and shakes her head.

"The name does sound sort of familiar. Why?"

"She went to your school. Would be the same age as you. Even in some of your classes?"

"Nah, I know everyone in my classes. Why, Dad?"

Dawson struggles to think of the right way to put this.

"Er… I wanted to talk to you earlier… But you know how your mother has banned all work-related topics from the dinner table?"

She chuckles. The girls had loved their father's stories. So much so that Dawson sometimes got too into them and started revealing information too sordid for their young ears, and Helen had banned all matters of work stories from the dining room table.

"Well… Jill Yates was the girl found dead this morning. We believe she's been murdered."

Alicia's smiling mouth instantly drops into a gaping hole of horror.

"We're looking to talk to anyone we can who may have information on her. I was just wondering whether you could lead me in the right direction?"

"No, Dad. Sorry. I wish I could, but I never knew the girl. I might recognise her name, but I can't put a face to it. Is that why the police were at our school today? My mates have been texting me, telling me I missed all the madness. How come it hasn't been all over the news?"

"We've been keeping it hush hush. Most journalists know that a young girl's body has been found, but don't know who just yet. But it will be all out in the open tomorrow. The Herald contacted us earlier asking for a quote. I don't know how they know, but they do. DS Simpson said she had to chase a journalist from the house of the people that found the body earlier. So you're going to hear tomorrow anyway. The police have just spoken to teachers and a few friends of Jill's. They should be starting their interviews with individual students tomorrow. Just promise me that if you hear anything in school that you'll come straight to me?"

"I will, Dad. You know I will."

CHAPTER 22:

"Hon, what's happened?"

Roberta conceals her red blotched face with the shadows, slapping a finger to her lips, before sneaking down the corridor. She peers into the spare room, the blow-up bed still the only prominent thing in the whole place. There lies Lydia, snoozing lightly. Roberta turns and jumps with fright. Jeff hadn't made a sound the whole journey after her. He mouths '*what's wrong*?' Roberta shakes her head and points towards their bedroom door.

"Bastards," Jeff says, shaking his head after Roberta lets him in on the events of her visit home.

"I know, they'll never change," Roberta buries herself in Jeff's old university hoody, her favourite. It has makeup marks at the sleeves and is one of the few memorabilia left of Jeff's uni days, but he knows how much she loves it and lets her sleep in it.

"You need to ring the social."

"I don't know, Jeff."

"What do you mean '*you don't know*?'"

"I lived there too, you know? I was once the one getting taken off them and put into foster care. Some families were okay, don't get me wrong. But the majority? Just saw me as damaged goods. Some only did it for the cash, or to prove their worth so maybe they could adopt their own one day. They all used me. I hated it. As much as I loathed living with my parents, it was familiar, you know? Living in a weird house in a scary neighbourhood when you didn't know your way around... It was terrifying. Especially at such a young age."

Jeff wraps his arms around her and rests his chin on her shoulder.

"I'm sorry, babe. I wish I knew you back then. I would've sneaked you into my room whenever my parents fell asleep."

They both laugh, finishing with a soft kiss. Jeff raises his eyebrows and sticks the tip of his tongue between his teeth.

"No way," she shrugs him off. "Not with her in the next room, and I haven't even finished my article yet."

He rolls his eyes dramatically, then smiles and squeezes her leg as she brings out the laptop from under the bed.

"So, what new information are you relaying to the masses tomorrow?"

"Well... Jill, the girl that was killed, had a secret boyfriend. The police are zoning in on him as we speak. Scott Woodhouse, he's called. Of course, I can't print the name in fear that he could go underground. So, looks like he's the prime suspect."

"Jesus," Jeff blinks a few times. "You got all this from the kid?"

"Not exactly," Roberta bites her lip. "The detective threw me out before I could get anything juicy. But..."

"But what?"

"I might've been a bit sneaky."

"How?"

"Well... She technically didn't escort me off the premises. She just closed the door in my face..."

Jeff's mouth falls open.

"You sat outside and listened in?"

Roberta shrugs.

"Roberta!"

"What? There's nothing illegal in a little eavesdropping. And it's not like I'm printing something that could jeopardise the case. Just adding a little more meat."

Jeff purses his lips and slips between the sheets, still clearly annoyed, but Roberta has no time in talking him around to the reporter's way of thinking. Some journos say the best thing to do is have a fellow journo as a partner. They understand what the other needs and wants. Even when stories come up, causing anniversary dinners to be ruined and them to be absent at family gatherings and important events. Roberta wonders what it would be like to have Jeff understand her every journalistic need whilst she waits for her e-mails to load, before she can continue on with the story she started at the office.

CHAPTER 23:

It's a little after 2am when Alicia creeps out of her room. She glances up and down the hallway to make sure it's deserted before pottering down the stairs, narrowly missing the step that creaks second from the bottom. She eases the key clockwise in the back door until she hears the thick click echo through the kitchen. As quietly as she can, she opens the door, slips herself out and delicately shuts it behind her. She wraps her cardigan around her to protect herself from the chilly night, before hopping onto the grass to mask her footsteps, despite her being in her bare feet. She can't be too careful.

She glides to the corner of the house, takes one last look up at the first-floor windows to make sure no lights greet her, and sneaks around the bins. She's met with complete darkness, the shadow of the house and next door's high fence shielding her from the bright moon. Bopping up and down to keep warm, she flicks her head left and right, wondering what side he'll come from.

Moments pass, before she hears the rattle on the gate.

"Sssh," she hisses, thrusting her finger to her lips, despite him not being able to see her yet. She slides the bolt back and winces as it's whine pierces the night. Satisfied that there is no movement coming from the house, she pulls the door open and smiles as Carl's face comes into view.

"Alright, babe?" he grunts, before leaning in to kiss her.

"Sorry about earlier," Alicia giggles as she pulls away seconds later. "My dad can be a bit of a schizo... But he means well."

"Whatever," he says before leaning in for another kiss.

Alicia giggles before pulling away again.

"Carl, stop it. My parents' room is just up there."

She turns to point towards the wall above where, behind inches of bricks and mortar, Dawson's headboard rests. But before she can turn around, Carl has dragged her in for a kiss again. Alicia starts to get uncomfortable and tries to pull away once more, but Carl's grip is too tight.

"Carl," she tries to speak, but her words are muffled by his tongue. He pushes his hands up her top and she tries to slap him away, but she's pressed hard against him and the wall, incapable of much movement.

"Carl, please, stop it," she moans through the thick saliva, tears springing to her eyes.

Carl breaks out of the kiss and shoves a hand over her mouth.

"Don't you dare scream."

Alicia blinks away the tears and looks at his face, but it's not Carl at all. It's Bobby Gardener. He pulls at her pyjama bottoms and she sobs into his gloved hand.

"I said shut up!"

He punches her with such force that she falls to the ground. Looking up, she sees Darren Ward towering over her, the same snarl prominent now as was on his custody picture. He proceeds to kick her in the stomach and she doubles over in pain. Her head ricochets back as the first blow connects with her chin. She lies on the cracked tiles in her garden and gazes up at her assailant, who is now shrouded in black apart from a white question mark hovering over his face. Still the hits come and come until Alicia feels like she may faint from the pain. Just as she's about to zone out, the boy leans forward from the darkness and she sees Jill Yates' face, all bruised and cut, but her eyes are open and she's very much alive.

Dawson jolts awake. He reaches for his bedside lamp to escape the shadows as his beating heart slows to normal. Peeling his sweaty back from the sticky sheets and making sure not to wake Helen, he steps out of bed and crosses the room to the hall. Satisfied that Alicia is safe in bed asleep, he shuffles down the stairs and out into the back garden. The gap between the bins and the gate is empty, spare for a few woodlice fleeing Dawson's feet. He trudges back into the kitchen and falls down on the stool, resting his head in his hands. Dragging them down his face to his chest, he sighs and looks at his reflection in the kitchen window, then out onto the far-off street. It's still early, and the cul-de-sac is quieter than ever.

"Where is this bastard now?" his voice, still croaky from sleep, vibrates off the white tiles and around the pristine kitchen, but isn't met with an answer.

CHAPTER 24:

"Sir, what are you doing?"

Simpson stands in the door frame of the incident room watching Dawson take down two of the four suspect pictures.

"I'm removing Kane Yates from our enquiries."

"But, sir-"

"He has a solid alibi with his wife and daughter. Even Kenny in The Rusty Crown has confirmed that he was there watching the football. We need to throw all our resources on our new leads."

"Sir, Donna is clearly terrified of him. You said yourself that Clara was uncomfortable when his name was breached. I don't trust him, sir. I think we should enquire more into his character-"

"Leave it, Simpson. Sure, the man may have a drinking problem, but name me ten people on Promised Hill that don't. He's clearly distraught and burdened with grief. He isn't acting himself, neither is the wife. We have to bring them justice.

And we'll do that by finding whoever killed Jill Yates."

Simpson's lips purse as Dawson slips the picture back into the incident file.

"I think you're making a mistake, sir. But so be it. Anyway, why are you removing Scott Woodhouse?"

"Because, Simpson…"

Dawson crumples up the substitute picture and aims it at the rubbish bin, narrowly missing. Shrugging off the setback, he sticks a fresh photo onto the board. It shows a man in his early-to-mid-twenties, a white builders hat covering his shoulder length blonde hair.

"Woodhouse?"

Dawson nods.

"DC Austin was able to track him down online. Works for Ribas Refurbishments. And guess what job the business is currently working on?"

Simpson's eyes expand.

"50 Connolly's Estate."

CHAPTER 25:

Ribas Refurbishments' office is situated in a retail park just south of the River Rong. However, despite the fancy big warehouses accommodating the Next and Argos stores, the officers are heading for a portacabin on the corner of the carpark. As Dawson pushes open the door, a selection of windchimes make their presence known. They look around at the bare white walls and tiles. The room is overpowered by a single counter enveloping the majority of the space, except for a small table with three cheap plastic chairs in the corner. The table is still littered with design ideas.

"The place is a bit plain to boast about their refurbishment skills," Dawson whispers from the corner of his mouth, forcing Simpson to suppress a smile.

"Ahhh, hallo, hallo. Come in my friends."

The detectives turn towards the counter, where a man is lifting the side flap to slide out and join them. He shakes their hands warmly with a huge grin on his face.

"Welcome to Ribas Refurbishments. My name is Ricardo Ribas. I'm manager here. Please – sit, sit."

He leads them over to the table and takes a seat facing them.

"You a lovely couple," he smiles again, nodding.

"Actually, Ricardo. We're not together."

The pair lean to one side of their chairs to pull their badges out of their back pockets. Upon observing their IDs, Ricardo's face drops.

"Maybe it's best we talk inside?"

"Ay, Díos mio. I know nothing about. You have to believe me."

Ricardo has been circulating his tiny office for the past few minutes. His Hispanic accent thicker now that he's floundering with his words.

"He was never left alone. Always supervised. There's no way. Oh, que es lo que voy hacer?"

"Ricardo, please, sit down."

Ricardo returns to his seat, repeating '*joder*' under his breath.

"Tell us what you know about Scott Woodhouse."

Ricardo shrugs.

"He's been working for me a few years now. I thought he had promising career. Always gives one hundred percent. Hasn't called in sick one time."

"And were you ever at 50 Connolly's Estate?"

"Of course. A few time. To overlook progress. It was real mess when we started. Not lived in in years. Mouldy. Some homeless staying there for few nights. I told landlord it would take three or four month at least."

"And who was in charge of the operation?"

"Oh, me, me, me, me. I tell everyone what needs done and they do it."

"And what was... *Is* Scott working on?"

"He's working on downstairs back. Kitchen and garden."

"Is he there now?"

"No. Holiday days since Friday."

"Do you know where he is, Ricardo?"

CHAPTER 26:

Scott Woodhouse crosses the landing to the phone in his flat's hallway. Pressing the video button, he's met with the very pixilated bald head of a middle-aged man. Confused, he lifts the receiver.

"Hello?"

"Scott Woodhouse?"

"Yeah?"

"Can you let me in please?"

"Err... Who's this?"

"I'm Detective Inspector Donald Dawson. My colleague here is Detective Sergeant Jade Simpson."

He flashes his badge in front of him, about thirty degrees the wrong way from the camera.

"We'd like to ask you a few questions."

"Er... Okay, I'll buzz you in."

Moments later, the detectives are seated on Scott's uncomfortable sofa.

"We're here to talk about your relationship with Jill Yates," Simpson cocks her head to the side.

Scott's face automatically falls.

"Er... Who?"

"Nice try. Look... We don't care about the age gap... For now. So unless you want arrested on paedophile charges, I'd start talking."

"Alright, alright," Scott is physically shaking as he rubs his mouth. "What do you want to know?"

"Starting from the start would be nice," Simpson's eyes narrow.

"Well, we were called in to refurbish a house on Connolly's Estate-"

"Number 50?"

"Yeah. Must be a few months ago now, when-"

"We're going to need exact times here, Mr Woodhouse."

"Oh. Well, it was our first project after the new year. So... Say the second week in January?"

He gazes at the officers before Dawson gives him a slight nod to let him continue.

"Well, when we got there, the place was a mess. A right dump. I mean, I've been working with the refurb company for a few years now, but this was one of, if not *the* worst. Anyway, one day, a few weeks in, I was working on the garden. Pulling out weeds, fixing broken slabs. I looked up and saw Jill looking out of her bedroom window down towards me. When she saw that I noticed her, she quickly pulled her blinds. This went on for a while... Maybe two or three days. Looking back now, I should've known she's just a school girl. I never saw her before 4 o'clock, but I just thought maybe that was the time she worked to. I mean, she never had a school uniform on, I swear."

He holds both hands up in the air.

"Well obviously, after so much work with planting new pots and redesigning the layout and putting down new tiles and patios, there was nothing more I could do to the back yard. So I started on the kitchen. From there, I could still see into her bedroom through the window. With a few extra panes of glass, she seemed to be confident enough to not shut her blinds. She watched me working, but when I went outside to get supplies or have a fag, she hid away. Finally, a few days after this charade, I waved to her and she waved back. I pointed to the garden and she shrugged before smiling. I came out for a fag a few minutes after and she didn't close her blinds. I said hello to her, and she responded. I made small chat about the weather and she shyly started to respond through the open window."

He bites his lip as he concentrates on the memory.

"This continued until one time when I pointed at the garden, by the time I was out there, she wasn't at the window. I continued my fag before I realised that she was on the other side of the fence from me. I heard the soft breathing first, and when I said hello she squealed with delight. She didn't speak after that. By the time I got back to the kitchen, she was back at the window. Think she ran off. The next time she squeaked a hello back. Over the next few days, we started chatting more. She seemed to warm to me. Get a little more comfortable. Sometimes I would bunk off work to have a quick fag and a smidge of conversation with her. She was very shy, but you could tell she was so smart. And didn't act like someone underage at all. I didn't know that until later on. I just thought she was playing hard to get. *Very* hard to get. Fed up with the games one Friday night, I asked her out and she said yes. I took her out to a restaurant and things escalated from there."

"When did you find out she was only 15?" Simpson asks.

"Just last week. She finally admitted it to me. I haven't seen her since."

"So you called it off?"

Scott bites his lip.

"Not formally, no. But I wasn't planning on taking her out again."

"How physical was your relationship?"

"I kissed her a few times. But that was it. She never wanted anything more. And once I found out, I was glad that we didn't take it further."

"How did you not know she was underage?"

He shrugs.

"She didn't look it. Didn't act like it."

"Did she have wine with dinner?"

Even Dawson gives Simpson a confused look.

"Er... No."

"Anything alcoholic?"

"No."

"Didn't you find that strange?"

"At first... But then I asked her if she drank and she said she didn't. Said she watched her mum and dad devote their lives to it so she swore off the stuff."

"And the way she went on before you dated her?"

"What about it?"

"Didn't you find it a tad... Childish?"

"Well... Yeah, looking back now. But I've went out with girls who were weirder."

"All legal, I presume?"

"Yes," Scott's face is like thunder.

"So when is the last time you made contact with Miss Yates?" Dawson takes over, feeling Scott's detest start towards Simpson.

Scott blows a raspberry whilst in thought.

"Last week sometime, through the window in her bedroom."

"We're going to need to know an exact date."

"Must've been Wednesday."

"And when exactly did you find out about the age gap?"

"The night before."

"And how did that conversation go?"

"Not good."

"Mr Woodhouse, we need details."

"Alright. I told her I needed some time to think, but I knew it wasn't right. She's too young."

"And she took it bad?"

He shrugs again.

"I guess she was a little upset."

"Where did this conversation take place?"

"In the alley linking the houses. Towards the end we met there a few times."

The two detectives share a concerned glance, which Scott picks up on.

"What?"

"You took your holiday on the Friday?" Dawson ignores him.

"Yeah, what about it?"

"What about the Thursday? Didn't you see Jill then?"

"No. I took a half day. Was out of there by lunchtime. She wouldn't have been home from school," he says bitterly.

"Mr Woodhouse, Jill's body was found in the alley behind her house early yesterday morning. We believe she has been murdered. Where were you in the late hours of Sunday night and early hours of yesterday morning?"

Scott stares at the detectives open mouthed, before stammering.

"Wh – You – Who... You can't think this was me? What happened? What..."

He takes a minute to process this, his head in his hands, before jerking up.

"This wasn't me. You don't understa-"

"Where were you, Scott?"

"Here, I was here."

"Were you alone?"

"Yeah, I live alone."

"Bit of a coincidental time to take your holidays, wouldn't you say Mr Woodhouse?" Simpson purses her lips.

"I booked my holidays months in advance," Scott growls.

"Funny how you knew yesterday was a bank holiday and you-"

"Yesterday wasn't a bank holiday," Scott mutters, his face in a snarl. Dawson looks at her with raised brows.

"Oh, wasn't it?" Simpson looks confused. "Well, when I was doing door-to-door questioning yesterday, I knocked on number 50 and no one answered. Care to explain that? I thought your team would still be helping out at the house?"

Scott shrugs.

"Maybe they had left already?"

"At lunchtime? No, I'm sure your entire team don't head home before their sandwiches."

The shade on Scott's face darkens.

"No, Mr Woodhouse. Because Ribas Refurbishments was closed yesterday. Wasn't it?"

Scott protrudes his lip.

"I don't see why they would be?"

"No? Where is Ricardo Ribas from, Mr Woodhouse?"

"Up near Evergreen."

"No, where is he from originally?"

"Well, that's a bit racist."

"Is he Spanish, Mr Woodhouse?"

"Clearly."

"I don't know if DI Dawson would agree with me, Mr Woodhouse, but when we paid Mr Ribas a visit this morning, he was looking a bit rough. Like he'd been drinking yesterday."

Scott shrugs again.

"And I couldn't help but notice a wedding ring on his finger. He is married, I presume?"

"Yes."

"Children?"

"Yeah, three. One on the way"

"And I also saw a sign on the counter. One that looked like it had just been taken down. Do you know what that sign said, Mr Woodhouse?"

Scott doesn't dare avert his eyes from Simpson's stare, like a mad dog about to pounce on its prey.

"It said '*Sorry, we're closed today. El Dia del Padre.*' Do you know what that means, Mr Woodhouse?"

"Something about a father?"

"Correct. Now my O Level Spanish might not be up to scratch, but I think it loosely translates to '*Father's Day.*' My friend's husband is from Malaga. Although he has no children, he has a lot of friends who do. So he was, like Mr Ribas, out yesterday celebrating Saint Joseph's Day. The two coincide, but I'm sure you knew that."

"I didn't."

"Don't play dumb with me, Mr Woodhouse. You took your holidays and knew that the office, and therefore, number 50 Connolly's Estate would be empty on Sunday March 18th and Monday March 19th. Why, Mr Woodhouse, may I ask?"

"I genuinely have no idea what you're talking about. You have no evidence to suggest that I had any part in this murder. Now, unless you're going to arrest me, I would appreciate it if you left my flat. Immediately."

CHAPTER 27:

"Who is it?"

Roberta can hear Kane shout from the living room. The FLO smiles awkwardly.

"I don't know if I can let you in. Police business."

"Have the police not already taken statements?"

"Yes, but-"

"Well, in case you haven't seen the Herald this morning, or the news throughout today, Jill's name has been released. Now, I may be the first, but I certainly won't be the last to be knocking on this door today. So, either you can let me in now and I can interview the parents, and by publishing this new information, that will discourage anyone else from coming to the door. Or you can be bombarded with requests from journalists from around the country."

The FLO's eyes widen. Amateur, she knew it.

"Around the country?"

"Yes, this case seems to have high public interest. We've just started to see other journos arriving at hotels in the town centre. I'm sure it'll be no time before the-"

"Whoever it is, tell them to hurry up and come in and shut the door," Kane barks.

The FLO, now introducing himself as Nick, smiles and shakes Roberta's hand. Within minutes, she's parked herself in front of the remaining Yates family, Nick perched awkwardly by her side.

"She was a lovely girl," Kane nods, holding his wife's hand a little too tight. "Always smiling. Always laughing. I just wish we could find the bastard who did this to her."

The little girl, Clara, flinches at the expletive as it's spat.

"I understand, Mr Yates. And that's why your statements will get the community talking. Hopefully raise morale and get them thinking. Someone somewhere is bound to know something to get whoever is responsible caught. Never underestimate the power of the press," she smiles.

The family are silent.

"Clara, sweetie, what do you miss most about your sister?" Roberta leans forward and smiles at the cute little girl.

"Wow, excuse me, what are you doing?" Kane's huge hand covers most of the child's face as he levers himself off of the sofa.

"I just wanted to speak to Cl-"

"Don't you dare speak to my daughter. She's only a littlun."

"I apologise, Mr Yates. I just thought-"

"Well you thought wrong. We've changed our minds. I want no such interview. Now, if you don't mind, I want you to leave this house before I call DI Dawson."

"And then he slammed the door in my face."

Roberta sits at her desk, several nosy colleagues crowded around listening to the hot gossip from her latest visit to Connolly's Estate. Budds hasn't uttered a word since she started, he has just sat and chewed his pen. When the gatherers have shared their two pennies' worth, he retracts the pen before speaking.

"Well, there's nothing we can do about that. Maybe find out if there's any other relatives... Teachers... Friends... Anything to build a sense of community in the article. I'm sure you'll put your own spark to it regardless."

Roberta fails to hide her blush.

"Thanks, Budds."

"And well done on this morning. We were wondering how long it would take DS Simpson to phone in."

"She did?"

"She did. Gave old Mary on the phones a right ear shattering telling off. Well done."

"Well done?"

"Of course. The public want answers, Roberta. And they're not getting them from the police. Your story has got people talking. Got people angry. Emotions are high. And we have one up from any other newspaper in the country. All those people camping out outside the Gardener's. They don't have half as much as our Roberta," he winks at her. "Now, everyone, back to work. Barry, I hope you have got contact with that-"

The semi-circle of people around Roberta's desk slowly disperse, leaving her alone. She bites the inside of her mouth in thought. No one told her she did the right thing. No one told her to ignore Kane Yates and that he was just angry with grief or troubled from the experience. She's a big girl now, she doesn't need constant reassurance, but something about being on the end of that man's acrimony had unsettled her deeply.

CHAPTER 28:

Just shy of five o'clock and officers at Rong Valley's Police Department are already packing up their things and heading home after a very unsuccessful day. Hoping that tomorrow will bring new leads and answers to the ever-growing questions throbbing around the station. Dawson is slumped in an office chair in the incident room, hoping that if he spreads the disarranged files across the huge table that something will blare out at him as if it were obvious. Alas, no such luck. After draining his numberless mug of coffee, he gazes out at the emptying office, as well as watching the approach of the returning Simpson.

"Any luck?" he asks as she flounces in.

"Nope. Cherrie has no idea where he is," she sighs as she flops herself down across the table from him.

Officers had visited Darren Ward's home, both yesterday and several times today.

"Charming as always," she sniffs.

"Does this make you worried?"

"A bit."

"We'll send uniforms over tomorrow, and if there's still no answer, then we'll station a few outside his house. He can't stay away forever. We've already been in contact with the airports, but he hasn't left the country. We have that to go on at least."

Simpson nods her head and brushes her fingers over the Herald's front page splashed out on the table beside her.

"Ignore it, Simpson."

"I can't help it. I should've known that she'd linger in the hallway."

"It's not your fault. I'm sure someone would've sniffed it out anyway. Regardless, there's no suspect name, so we were able to find Woodhouse, and it makes it sound like we've got a good grasp on the investigation."

"But we don't."

"Hey... You never know."

The two share tired glances before Simpson yawns and stretches.

"I'm going to head home here, mouths to feed," she smiles sweetly.

"Bright and early tomorrow," he wags a finger at her before returning the smile.

CHAPTER 29:

"No, for the last time, no work talk at the table."

Helen gives Dawson a look of death before crunching into her lettuce.

"Helen, this is a very import-"

"I don't give a fiddler's fart if it's important. You gave little Kyra here nightmares the last time you were talking business," she leans over to rub her youngest daughter's arm.

"That's different, this is-"

"I said no, Donald!" she hisses, tapping her fist on the table hard enough to cause a shake.

Their daughters look from one to the other like they're watching a very violent tennis tournament. Losing, Dawson returns his attention to Alicia and jerks his head towards the kitchen.

"I knew that I heard Jill's name somewhere before," Alicia says as she closes the door, but not before Dawson catches a glimpse at his wife's seething glare. "Bobby Gardener. He's this kid in our year, kind of keeps himself to himself. Doesn't really hang out with anyone. Except Jill. People say that he's in love with her. Well... *Was* in love with her. Used to follow her about school and always talk about her. My friends heard him talk about nothing else. Jenny caught him writing her initials with love hearts in the back of his lab book once in first year. People really slag him off, saying he's obsessed with her."

Dawson nods and considers this new information.

"Thanks, Leesh. Hopefully this is of some help."

"Be careful though. One boy called him out on it during PE one time a few years ago and he really went ape shi... Mad. Proper roaring and that. He's always got bullied. A bit of a weirdo. You don't know what he could be capable of."

CHAPTER 30:

"And what do you do if the nice policeman or woman come back?"

Kane has a firm grip on Clara's leg through her duvet.

"Say that I don't know where she is."

"Good. And when was the last time you seen her?"

"She put me to bed on Sunday night."

"And why can't you tell them that Daddy and Jill had a falling out?"

"'cause they'll think Daddy took her and they'll take Daddy away too."

"And you don't want that, do you?"

He increases his grasp and she winces with pain, but doesn't dare show any emotion.

"No, Daddy."

"Good girl."

And as quickly as the pain came, it's gone as he removes his hand. Tapping her cheek with a giant finger, he retreats out of Clara's room, before being met on the stairs by Donna.

"Where are you going?"

"Out."

"Where?"

"Does it matter?"

"Yes, K. It does. That liaison officer is gonna be back any minute and I don't know wh-"

"Oh, I'm sure you'll think something up. Plenty of inspiration."

He plugs one nostril with a finger and forces a sniff, moving his head from left to right.

"You bastard. Like you're any better."

"Yeah? Well at least I can get myself out of bed in the morning without a line."

"Oh I'm sure you couldn't if it weren't for the thought of the whiskey waiting for you at The Rusty Crown. Get off your high horse, you're just as bad as me if not wor-"

Kane thrusts his arm at Donna's neck until he's holding her against the wall, her feet centimetres from the steps. Beginning to choke, she looks down and frails her legs about wildly in an attempt to find a foothold. He edges his face closer to hers with a sneer. Last night's beer breath hot in her face.

"Don't you dare speak to me like that again, you hear me? You're nothing. A little maggot. Jill's better off without you as a mother."

The doorbell rings, but Donna continues to struggle, both hands around his arm trying desperately to pull him off. Seconds later, knocks follow at the door and just as Donna starts to see white, she falls to the ground. Kane thunders down the stairs and thrusts open the door.

"What?" he shouts.

Nick jumps with fright and drops one of his files.

"Oh, sorry Nick. Thought you were another rodent reporter."

"Don't worry, don't worry. No apologies needed. Good morning, Mr Yates. Let me just.." Nick fake laughs as he scoops up his notes before entering the open door.

Kane looks out at the collection of press already on the street and ignores their shouts and questions as he snaps the door shut. He thinks there's a half full bottle of JD in the cupboard. That'll have to mull him over until he can escape for a while.

CHAPTER 31:

Alicia's information about Bobby Gardener had brought no such luck to the investigation. Simpson returned to Windsor Place to further question him, but he was adamant that he had nothing to do with it. Both his parents confirmed that Bobby had only left the house on one occasion on Sunday, and that was for church that morning.

Scott Woodhouse's name got dragged through the dirt again and again. Dawson had contacted the landlord that owns the flat that Woodhouse lives in and asked for security tapes. Whilst leaving the premises the day before, Dawson had spotted three cameras. One beside the elevator and stairs leading onto Woodhouse's hallway, one when he came out of the elevator on the ground floor and one hovering over the front door. He received the footage this morning, and as he looks through it now, he sees that there is a further security camera at the back door fire exit, which had remained unopened all night, as well as one overlooking the lift on every floor.

"Any luck?"

Simpson pops her head into the ridiculous closet space that the station calls a studio.

"Nope."

Dawson rewinds the footage for Simpson's benefit. The screen, split into a dozen squares, shows people walking backwards through the lift and doors before he comes to a pause.

"Here," he presses play, jabbing his finger at the square on the top left-hand side of his screen, showcasing the footage from outside the front door of the apartment blocks. "You can see Woodhouse coming back from Tesco. He enters the lift," his finger moves slightly right as Woodhouse's head appears in the corner of the next window, before disappearing into the elevator. Moments later, he appears at the bottom right-hand screen, fighting with his pocket for the outcome of his keys.

"And he doesn't leave at all through the night?"

"Nope. Not until three in the afternoon the next day, Monday."

Simpson sighs dramatically, slumping herself in the chair next to him.

"I don't know what to tell you, sir. I thought I had it cracked... And Bobby Gardener seems unyielding."

"I know he does. Is there still no luck on the Darren Ward front?"

"No sir, but I have uniforms posted outside his house as we speak."

"Good. As awful as this sounds, his absence speaks wonders. Where is he? Why hasn't he come home? We need answers, and they could well and truly lead to Jill."

Simpson nods as they're interrupted by a knock at the door. An officer who looks more like he's here on work experience peeks his nose through the door.

"Sorry to bother you, detectives. But there's something I think you should see."

CHAPTER 32:

"He still won't leave his room," Mandy sighs as she returns to the kitchen table.

"Give him time, he's grieving," Dylan mutters over the sizzling of the half-prepared fry in the pan in front of him.

"He's hiding something."

"He's not."

"Dylan," Mandy stands up accusatorily, before composing herself. "He's not like this. This isn't our Bobby."

"His best mate's just died."

"It's not just that. You know he's been off with us for a while now, Dyl."

"He's a teenage boy, Mand," Dylan chuckles. "They don't like their parents at this age."

"He's always been fine with me. Just these past few months..."

Mandy trails off, gazing out of the kitchen window at the gate into the alley. The gate that, since being opened, has sent a hurricane through her family's lives. That's selfish, she thinks to

131

herself. If she's feeling like this, how in Hell are the Yates' feeling? Her thoughts are broken by the doorbell. She retreats down the hall and is met with the glum faces of DI Dawson and DS Simpson.

"Detectives. Nice to see you again. Bobby's in his room, I'll go-"

"No, Mandy. There's no need," Dawson crosses the threshold and looks the woman square in the eye. "We're here to see your husband."

CHAPTER 33:

"This is bullshit. You should be out trying to catch the killer of that little kiddie. Not traipsing through past files."

Dylan sits with his arms folded, facing the detectives in the harsh environment of Interview Room 1. Laid in front of the detectives are several battered looking files. Yellowing, dog-eared and coming up to 20-years-old.

"Mr Gardener, we believe you've been here before?"

"And what of it? Years before Jill Yates was even born. How have I been brought into this shit?"

"Mr Gardener, I'm going to ask you politely to watch your temper and your swearing," Simpson leans forward, her arms crossed. "We would like to ask you a few questions and the more cooperative you are, the smoother this interview will go. Okay?"

Dylan grumbles his agreeance.

"Now, Mr Gardener," Dawson takes over. "Can you please tell me what happened in the October of 1987 that resulted in your arrest?"

Dylan sighs and rubs his face.

"She was my girlfriend."

"Who was?"

"Sally-Anne."

"Sally-Anne Kennedy?"

"Yes."

"Go on."

"We were in a relationship. I was 16. She was 14. We both went to RV High. We were seeing each other for months. Yes, things got… Physical. It was completely consensual. We both wanted it. One night, we were at hers whilst her parents were out, but they landed back earlier than expected. Her dad caught us. I thought he was going to kill me, only I got out of there on time. The next day, the police were at my door. He'd filed a statutory rape allegation because she was underage."

Tears sting at Dylan's eyes, but he quickly wipes them away, refusing to show signs of weakness to the detectives.

"I got sent to juvie, but because of the length of my sentence, I had to spend some time in a proper prison. Only about six weeks or so. For that, it's been on my criminal record and I'm on the register. That's why I've always struggled to get jobs. That's why I have had to raise my Bobby in that shithole on Promised Hill. All because of that bastard. They moved away from Rong Valley by the time I was out. I've never had to see any of them, but I will *never* forgive him."

Dylan's lip wobbles with the pain of the memory, but still he holds his ground, seemingly transfixed on a point on the table.

"What sort of relationship did you have with Jill Yates, Mr Gardener?"

"I barely spoke to her. Like I've said before, she was very quiet. Only ever saw her when she was around with Bobby."

He looks up and moves his head from Dawson to Simpson and back again, taking turns leering into their eyes.

"I didn't do this. You have to believe me. I have no interest in kiddies. There's the same age gap between Mandy and I as there was between myself and Sally-Anne. Only this time, I made sure I was the youngster. It's nothing when you're this age. But back then... I didn't know it was a big deal. It had nothing to do with her age. We were young and dumb, thought we were in love. It was Sally-Anne as a person, nothing to do with her body."

Silence follows.

"Mr Gardener, you have to admit that it is a bit peculiar that it was *you* who found her body?" Simpson throws herself back in.

"I told you, it was Toby that found her."

"The dog?"

"Yes."

"Bit funny considering it can't talk or give a proper statement."

"Yet Mandy did. She told you that we were in bed and she asked me to go and see what he was barking at. That's when I found her."

"And where were you during the night, Mr Gardener?"

"In the house. I never left. Watched telly with Mandy and then we went to bed. Sundays are our lazy nights. We order a Chinese and don't leave unless we really need to."

"And she'll be able to confirm this alibi?"

"Of course. I'm sure she already has… Somewhere."

Dawson stops the tape and asks Dylan to wait there. The detectives leave the room and converse in the hall.

"I believe him," Simpson nods, gazing in at him through the small window.

"I'm not so sure."

"Sir?"

"A leopard never changes his spots, Simpson. I want to keep him in a while longer. Get uniforms to collect his computer. Search his house. Anything that could help us find that he's still into children."

"But, sir. There was no sexual connection with Jill's murder. Her hymen was still intact and there were no signs of oral or other physical insertion."

"Still, Simpson. Just because he didn't do anything doesn't mean that he didn't have any desire to."

"Do you think we'll get a warrant for a search?"

"I'll pitch it to the Super. If she's happy, then we'll dive in. All guns blazing."

CHAPTER 34:

Dawson sits in his study, head engulfed in the case files. There must be something he's missing. The Superintendent had quashed the DI's attempts for a search warrant on Dylan Gardener's house when Dawson approached her yesterday. She said there was insufficient evidence. She remembers the case from way back, and had been working on it herself for some time. She felt sorry for Gardener back then. Apparently, Sally-Anne Kennedy's father was a right tyrant. An upper-class snob who thought he owned every building and business he set foot in, including the police station. For that reason, she detested him from the beginning. She told Dawson that he was wasting his time with Gardener and to let him go.

Follow up leads were also dead ends. Bobby was still on the suspect list, but uniforms at the school interviewing friends and teachers didn't give any evidence to suggest that he was anything more than a love-struck teenager throwing a strop that the girl next-door overlooked him. Undercover officers followed Woodhouse for a while, but after countless shortcomings, they were pulled away for better use of their resources. Darren Ward was still a no show. The Super was even tempted to pull the surveillance over his house. Dawson thinks there's a few more good days in her before she lets them go too.

With Jill's funeral tomorrow, Dawson hopes that the killer might attend and give something away. The entire town had raised money for a proper burial. The Yates' weren't religious and didn't have a penny to their name to even bury their daughter in the back yard. Rong Valley's community came together to help them out. Dawson made sure that the person in charge of the fundraising organised the funeral proceedings, not wanting any of the money to go on any substances the parents might need to get through the next few days.

However, despite Dawson's best attempts, his name was still harsh on people's lips and thick with ink in the papers. Even laymen on the street were speculating about the DI. Wondering what has been taking so long to find the killer? What's he been doing? Further hearsay even included Dylan giving a spiteful exclusive to Roberta Holmes, the new crime editor of the Herald. He stated that because he was the one to find the body, he had been public enemy number one. Saying the detective was scraping the barrel. He had phoned and apologised before Dawson had left work earlier today, but the conversation was short lived.

Dawson's thought process is shattered with the knock on his office door. He fakes a smile as Alicia pops her head in.

"Alright, darling?"

"Fine, Dad. Just thought I'd let you know that Carl is on his way over. He'll be here shortly."

"Who?"

"Carl. My boyfriend. You asked me to invite him over for dinner, remember?"

Dawson closes his eyes and breathes out heavily. He had hoped that this case would've been shelved before he'd have to deal with this new drama. He spins his chair back around to his daughter.

"Right, sorry. There's been so much going on lately, I've completely forgotten. What time is he to arrive?"

"Well he texted me a few minutes ago to say he's just passing the park."

"Fine, fine. Well that gives me plenty of time to get a shower. I'll meet you downstairs, sweetheart."

CHAPTER 35:

Descending the stairs, Dawson pulls at the itchy jumper the in-laws had given him for Christmas. He hadn't had a chance to wear it yet, with no family functions starting until his own birthday in May. Dawson hopes that Jill's killer is rotting in a cell long before then. But for now, he tries to push work out of his mind as he'll have to grin and bear an awkward dinner with Alicia's new boyfriend. As he trots into the living room, his good shoes snapping on the tiles, he wonders why he even bothered to put them on. Carl sits on the settee with a pair of creased navy tracksuit bottoms and a stained green polo shirt with some brand name etched over the entire fabric. The detective looks down at his guest's scruffy trainers and grimaces.

"Carl, you nearly met Dad a few days ago," Alicia giggles.

Dawson braces himself to get ready to lift his arm and shake his hand, despite his disgust. But Carl merely glances up at him and nods, a bored expression painted on his face.

"Alright?"

"Fine, Carl. And yourself?"

He shrugs, returning his attention to the TV, scratching his unkept hair. Dawson bites his bottom lip. A Promised Hill inhabitant. Lounging on his sofa. Watching his TV. Dating his daughter. His blood starts to boil.

"Don't judge a man," he whispers to himself, before repeating it over and over again until he hitches up his cords and takes a seat, pulling the pouffe over next to his new least favourite couple. "So, Carl. How's school?"

Carl grunts in amusement and shares a glance with Alicia.

"What?" Dawson narrows his eyes at the pair.

"Dad, you're so boring. You don't have to talk to him about school," Alicia giggles, squeezing the boy's leg.

Probably because he hasn't gone in years, Dawson thinks to himself.

"Oh, sorry. Do you work then?"

Again with the shrug, making Dawson believe his previous opinion was correct. He doesn't go to school and he doesn't have a job. And here he is, living it up in his living room.

"Carl works at a club in town, Dad."

"Oh, really? Which one?"

"Bar Boss."

Dawson finds it hard to hide the revulsion from his face. Bar Boss. Also known as '*the drug hole*,' in the station. And this new information means that his fears are correct. Carl would have to be at least 18 to work in there. A legal man with his 15-year-old girl.

"I know it well. Bartender?"

"Only on weekends," Carl extends his arms in a yawn and inches down the sofa more, until his head is almost level with the arm rest. His t-shirt riding up and showing his boxers, which are far higher than his bottoms.

"And on the weekdays?"

Dawson's starting to get angry with the shrugs.

"See if any jobs need doing around the streets."

"That's nice," Dawson nods, deciding to ignore the fact that he just described a prostitute. "Painting fences, fixing washing machines. That kind of help?"

"Yeah, sure."

Alicia looks from her dad to her boyfriend with a look of pride and bliss. Dawson coughs and groans as he stands.

"Gonna go in and see if your mother needs any help with dinner. Stew okay for you, Carl?"

"Whatever, Mr D."

Dawson bites his tongue and winces as he turns the corner into the kitchen, snapping the door shut behind him.

"Well, have you met Prince Charming?"

Helen peels herself away from the cooker long enough to give her husband a quick peck on the lips, it's the first time she's seen him since this morning.

"Prince Charming? Prince Charming? You've got to be joking?"

"Sshh," Helen whispers, turning the ladle in her signature huge pot. "What's wrong with him?"

"What's right with him? Did you see what he was wearing? And his attitude? What the hell does Leesh see in him? I don't think I can make it through dinner. I don't know if I want him in this house, never mind within ten feet of our daughter-"

"Don, please." Helen wraps her arms around his shoulders. "I know it's stressful seeing your baby girl with another man, but you have to get used to it. God, with your little princess, Sue, I thought you were going to be locking yourself in your cells for the night," she laughs.

"Sue was different. She never brought home rubbish like that-"

"Donald!"

"Sorry, but it's true."

"Honey, she could bring back a banker with tonnes of money or a straight A student or... Daniel bleedin' Radcliffe and you still wouldn't be happy. You're finding all his flaws. You need to switch yourself off," she presses her fingers against his temple. "Promise me something. When we sit down to dinner, pick out three things that are good about him. Things you like. Will you do that for me?"

Dawson sighs and sits on the kitchen stool, too mentally drained and hungry to argue anymore.

"Fine."

The couple sit in silence for a few seconds whilst Helen adds flavouring to her famous stew.

"Who's Daniel Radcliffe?"

CHAPTER 36:

Roberta sits in her car down the street from her parents' house. She's been here for ten minutes and can't bring herself to get out and march up to the door. Not yet, anyway. What will she say? Will it even make a difference?

She was waiting to hear back from an important source when her phone rang earlier. Instantly picking it up without checking the caller ID, she was confused to hear a stranger's voice on the other end.

"Hello there. Is this Roberta Holmes?"

"It is... Who's calling?"

"It's Sylvia from Rong Valley Primary School. I'm sorry to bother you Miss Holmes, but it's about your sister, Lydia."

"Is she okay?" Roberta had started to panic.

"Yes, yes. She's fine. She's fine. We've tried to contact your parents on several occasions, but their phone just cuts out. Your number is the alternative, I'm afraid."

"Don't worry, what's wrong?"

"I think it's best you come in. The principal is looking a word."

Sylvia was equally as lovely in person when Roberta travelled into the school. The principal wasn't. Mr Watkinson's bald head reflected the glare from the huge ceiling light, making Roberta struggle to observe him without straining her eyes.

"Your sister was in detention today for fighting," he said, almost bored, as soon as her cheeks touched the seat in front of his desk. Not one for small talk.

"What? Lydia? Fighting? There must be some mistake, she's so timid and-"

"Yeah, yeah. That's what they all say. I'm sure at home she's lovely and timid, but on the playground today, she bit a fellow pupil."

Roberta had looked at him with shock etched across her whole face.

"She *bit* someone?"

"Yes."

She had struggled for words after that. Too confused and shocked to register what the principal was saying. She had to ask him to repeat, much to his annoyance.

"Of course, I would prefer it if I was speaking to your parents, but I've never actually met them. They never show up to collect her or for parent-teacher meetings. Some excuse or another always arises. Anyway, that's irrelevant. What we need is to discuss Lydia's development. She can't go around biting my students, Miss Holmes."

"I completely understand."

"Therefore, I've gave her detention until the end of next week. I'm sure you, or your parents, will want to further punish her on your own terms. But may I suggest a non-violent approach? She's at a critical age and we would appreciate it if you dealt with her accordingly."

"Meaning?"

For once, the principal looked uncomfortable. He played around with a few sheets on his desk before coughing and continuing.

"I'm just saying that subjecting her to further violence isn't good. I don't know where she's got the habit of biting people out o-"

"It's not a habit. This is an isolated offence."

"I hope so, Miss Holmes. All I'm saying is she hasn't learned that from my school. Whether she's been playing video games or watching movies beyond her age range, or if there's trouble at hom-"

"I can assure you that there isn't."

He looked at her confused.

"I thought you didn't live with her?"

"I don't. But I'm around often enough. She's just going through a phase. I'll talk to her. See what was bothering her. I apologise again, Mr Watkinson."

She hadn't wanted to escape from a room as fast as she did back then.

CHAPTER 37:

Taking a deep breath, Roberta climbs out of her car and up the drive of her old house.

"Twice in one week, to what do we owe the pleasure?" her mum tuts, inhaling another cigarette.

Lydia hugs Roberta as she enters the living room.

"Lyd, can you do me a massive favour?"

"Sure, Robby."

"Jeff is working late tonight. And I watched a scary film last night. I'm too afraid to stay on my own, will you keep me company? Just for tonight?"

Lydia's eyes light up as she hops up and down, giggling excitedly.

"Oh, can I Mummy? Please, please, please?"

Janine hasn't been listening. Halfway through filling up her glass with vodka, she turns to the girl.

"What are you talking about? Calm down you're giving me a migraine."

"Can I stay with Robby tonight, please?"

Janine shrugs and leans back on the sofa, flicking her flipflops off and resting her grubby feet on the coffee table, narrowly missing the vodka bottle.

"Quick, run up and get your stuff," Roberta ruffles Lydia's hair, before watching her sprint out of the room and up the stairs. She mentally pictures the girl running across the landing, following the thunder of her feet with her head. Satisfied that she's in her room collecting her things, her eyes revert to her parents on the sofa.

"Dad, wake up," she kicks him in the shin.

Ian lurches awake, wiping the saliva from his chin.

"What the fuck are you do-"

"No, I talk. You two listen. I was called into Lydia's school today. They've been trying to contact you, why haven't you answered the phone?"

The couple's eyes rest on the carpet, where their phone lies, before following the cord until it disappears under the sofa. Roberta steps on the line and flicks it backwards. Surely enough, out comes the end of the line, nowhere near the wall in the hall where it should be plugged in.

"What did I do to deserve such useless parents?"

"Don't speak to me like that in my own house," Ian stands up and squares up to his daughter. "You might think you're some big shot with your new house and your fancy job, but you're never old enough to get a smack about the head."

Roberta doesn't break his stare, pushing her shoulders back to make herself look taller.

"I've just been to the school. They say that Lydia is in detention until the end of next week."

"Good enough for her," Janine snorts.

"She was fighting in school. Bit one of her peers. I wonder where she could've got such an idea from?"

Ian chuckles and rests himself back on the sofa.

"Nothing to do with us."

"It has everything to do with you. You're her parents. You're supposed to be bringing her up properly. Not teaching her to do things like that!"

"We never taught her to do anything. What? You think we asked her to go in and bite the first person she sees?"

"She's learning violent behaviour in her own home. Where she should feel safe. You may have fucked up your own lives, and tried to fuck up mine. But I'm not going to let you fuck up Lydia's."

Roberta opens her mouth to say more, but stops once she hears footsteps on the stairs. Turning and smiling at Lydia, she leads her out of the house and down the drive before her parents have any idea what's happened.

CHAPTER 38:

"I hope you like stew, Carl," Helen sings as she folds herself into the chair opposite him.

"Cheers, Mrs D," Carl says as he heaps his first forkful and shoves it into his mouth.

Dawson glares across the table at him, before winching at the light kick his wife gives him below the table. Smiling in apology to Helen, he glances back at Carl. He has a strong jawline, he thinks, as Carl devours the meal. Could that be a positive? Dawson thinks not, as he watches Carl attack his food without taking a breath. Like a hungry carnivore wolfing down a carcass. He looks like he hasn't eaten in Christ knows how long. Then Dawson remembers, he probably isn't used to a big dinner like this.

"You like your food then, Carl?" he nods.

Carl does the irritating shrug that Dawson hopes is just a nervous twitch.

"In our house… Our motto is… Eat or go hungry," he says through chews. "So many brothers… Growing men… My mum calls us… Too many mouths to feed… Not enough food in the

154

fridge... Sometimes I'd go to bed without any dinner."

"Well there's plenty of leftovers, so don't worry about having to leave with an empty belly," Helen shines a smile towards him.

"Yeah, no need to eat like a dog from a bowl," Dawson sniffs.

Alicia drops her fork on her plate with a dramatic clunk.

"Dad!"

"What?"

"Don't be so rude."

"All I'm saying is he looks like he hasn't seen food in a while. Your mother said there's plenty there. No need to rush."

Both Alicia and Helen purse their lips in disgust, whilst Kyra leans forward and giggles at her father, thinking she's being discreet. Dawson narrows his eyes in a playful way at his daughter. A 'we'll talk about this later' signal. Their connection is broken with the irritating sound of the new Nokia ringtone. Carl fidgets under the table and brings out his mobile.

"Alright, Fishy?"

Dawson grimaces. Fishy? What kind of boy is called Fishy? Helen's smile doesn't fade as she stares at Carl, but her eyes are strained. She hates anyone using their phone when they sit down for dinner nearly as much as she hates work talk.

"Yeah, yeah. I know."

He raises his eyes from the plate and realises that everyone at the table is staring at him.

"Look, I'll call you later, yeah? Good man."

And as quickly as the ringtone pierced the silence, the phone is snapped shut and replaced in his pocket. Unbeknown to Carl, he picks up his knife and fork and goes back to his dinner. As if nothing ever happened.

"So, Mr D...."

Dawson flinches at his new unwanted nickname once again.

"... How's this murder investigation going?"

Dawson eyes him suspiciously before Helen stutters into the conversation.

"Sorry, Carl. But we don't discuss work at the table. Not while we're eating."

"Oh. Sorry Mrs D, I just wanted to see what the famous Detective Inspector Dawson thought of the biggest case to hit Rong Valley in centuries. Isn't that what the press are calling it?" Carl smirks distinctly at Dawson.

"Yeah, well whether the journalists are saying that or not, I still don't allow that kind of discussi-"

"Why are you so interested, Carl?" Dawson puts down his cutlery and folds his hands together, his chin resting on them.

"No reason," Carl's lip protrudes, but his eyes don't leave the face of the lead detective. "Just being nosy, is all. See all sorts around my parts. I live about a five minute walk from where the girl was found. Just wanted to know the word on the street, so to speak."

Carl raises his eyebrows so imperceptibly that Dawson has to guess whether he imagined it or not.

"Well, I'd love to hear your side of things, Carl-"

"No, not tonight. Not at the table. You all know the rules. No work talk at the table. We can't overlook the rule because we have a guest. If anything, the rule should be enforced even more. Now, Carl, how are your spuds?"

CHAPTER 39:

"Now, then..."

Roberta gently closes the door to her flat and turns to see Lydia's massive smile light up her living room. Her tiny hands clasped around her overnight bag.

"You run and put your pjs on and I'll make you some hot chocolate."

Moments later, Lydia enters the kitchen in her pyjamas, shyly biting her nails.

"Come on, up on the stool," Roberta pats the plastic space beside her.

But Lydia won't move.

"What's wrong, Lyd?"

She shakes her head.

"Come on, tell me. Please?"

Lydia removes her finger but visibly bites her lip. Roberta hops off her own stool and crosses the room, bending down on her haunches to come level with her younger sister. After a few seconds of goading, Lydia leads Roberta by the hand into her spare room.

"What is it?"

Lydia's eyes fill with tears as she drags the duvet off the blow-up mattress, still inflated from her previous stay, and onto the floor. There, on the shoddily spread sheet, lies a deep yellow stain. Roberta looks from the stain to her sister, and it takes her longer than she'd like to admit to register what is going on.

"Oh, Lyd. Is that what you're worried about? I have more sheets. Come on and we'll throw these in the washing, won't we?"

She bunches up the sheets and wraps them around her sister's discarded pyjamas and underwear, lying at the foot of the mattress with similar stains.

"You're not angry?"

"Why would I be angry?"

"Mummy and Daddy get angry when it happens at home."

"Well, I'm not Mummy or Daddy. It's perfectly natural. But, just in case, we'll maybe give the hot chocolate a miss tonight, yeah?"

CHAPTER 40:

"Well, that was a fucking disaster."

Dawson has joined his wife in the kitchen as she's just finishing off the dishes stocking up her sink.

"It wasn't that bad."

"He's a rodent, Helen. And I plan on spraying this entire house with repellent."

"Now, Don. Don't be mean. He..."

She bites her tongue as she thinks, pretending to be focused on a stubborn stain on one plate.

"He... He seems to like our daughter. That's all that matters."

"How old is he?"

Helen looks at him confused.

"Pardon?"

"He works in a bar. No, not just any bar. Bar Boss of all places. The dive just off Chessington Street. You know, the one the druggies go to? The one my officers are called out to almost every weekend and Wednesday night."

"Times are hard, Don. Everyone needs all the jobs they can get. That doesn't mean that he does drugs."

"I beg to differ," Dawson grunts, forcing himself onto a stool to prevent himself from his inevitable pacing.

"Look, he seems to make our daughter happy," Helen wraps her arms around Dawson's neck, her sud-soaked hands stretched out, away from his clothing. "As long as he makes her happy, there's nothing we can do. Even the famous Detective Inspector Dawson," she smirks.

"Yeah, what was that about?" he jumps up from his seat and gently removes her arms from around him, much to her disappointment. "That was weird. Him looking into the investigation. I wonder if he has anything to do with it? Very fishy... And Fishy! That lad that rang him. Who names their son Fishy for Christ's sake?"

"Well, I'm guessing that's the nickname his friends have given him."

"And a scummy nickname at that. Why would you want people to call you something like that? I'd stamp that right out. You can tell a lot about someone from the friends they hang around with, Hel. Take it from me, I've been in the business long enough."

BRADD CHAMBERS

Helen rolls her eyes and returns to the dishes, half listening to her husband's latest repugnant rant.

CHAPTER 41:

Carl finally gets a quiet moment when Alicia slides off to the toilet, but not before kissing him three or four times, leaving him with a craving in her wake. He pulls out his phone and sends a quick text before silently breaking out of the front door. As he crosses the grass, he takes a look up and down the street. They're not here. Shit!

Taking a quick glance behind him to make sure no one from the Dawson family have their face painted against the windows, he jogs down the street a bit. That's when he sees the old Peugeot flash its lights at him. He waves and the passenger door opens. Out steps Fishy. As he reaches him, Carl extends his shaking hands.

"Hurry up, her old man is a cop."

Fishy plonks a wad of notes in his outstretched hand and is quickly reimbursed with a fistful of pills.

"You took these into a copper's house?" Fishy raises his hands to eye level. "You really are mad," he chuckles, his thick London accent piercing the cold air.

He takes another drag of his joint before offering the remnants to Carl. Carl gratefully accepts, hurries some parting words and retreats back towards the Dawson's house. Inhaling fast, Carl flicks the butt into the open drain before turning up the drive, only to come face to face with the DI himself.

"Shit, Mr D. You scared me."

Dawson glares at him unsatisfied, before following the noise of the Peugeot spluttering to life. It revs its engine and speeds off, sounding more like a motorbike than a shitty car. Dawson returns his gaze to Carl.

"Friends of yours?"

"Nah, erm… Yeah. Well, sort of. Boys I know from work."

Carl's thankful that he's downwind from the detective, knowing that he was stupid to accept a spliff when he hadn't any deodorant to mask the stench.

"Lovely boys, I presume?" Dawson smirks.

"Er… Yeah. Well I've just really recently got to know them, ya know?"

Carl tries to squeeze past the detective and the gate, but the burly man is making it impossible to step onto his property.

"Saw you having a little fag there. You wouldn't happen to have another, would you? I

164

stopped years ago, but... You know? What the wife doesn't know won't hurt her," Dawson chuckles.

"No, Mr D. Sorry. I don't. One of the lads just left me his ends. I try not to do it too often. Only when I'm drinking or..."

"Stressed?"

Carl smirks again.

"Yeah. You could say that. You know? Meeting the in-laws."

"You know you've said more to me in these past few seconds than you have all night, Carl?"

"Have I? Must just be getting to know you a little better, Mr D. Not as nervous," he gives a wheezy laugh.

"Or you're hiding something..."

The pair stare at each other for a while longer before Carl bursts into fake laughter.

"Me? Hide something? I'm an open book."

Dawson joins in on the laughter for a few seconds, before stepping forward, his shadow enveloping Carl from the light of the moon.

"I know exactly what you're like, son. I've dealt with plenty of your crowd and I'm sure I will deal with a few more in my line of work. Now, I saw exactly what happened here. So, I could arrest you. Take you up for possession, supply and use. Or..."

Carl's eyes had been rooted to the floor, but with the presentation of an ultimatum, his eyes shoot towards the detective's face excitedly.

"You leave. Don't contact my daughter ever again. I don't want you anywhere near her or any of the rest of my family. You hear me?"

Carl considers this with bated breath, before nodding forcefully.

"Good, now go!"

Dawson didn't shout, but the force of his voice makes the words echo across the street and around and around Carl's head as he jogs away.

CHAPTER 42:

"Rob, it's not normal for a seven-year-old to still be wetting the bed," Jeff is just back from a long day at work and sighs as he melts onto their own mattress.

"Are you sure? I've been googling and it seems to be common in children going through stress, such as bullying or moving to a new school."

"Well... It seems that your Lydia is the one doing the bullying," Jeff chuckles, but stops as soon as he sees his fiancé's glare.

"It's growing up in that house, Jeff. She's stressed out. Christ, I was only there for a few minutes today and they stressed me out. I can't imagine what it would be like to live with them again. Have they got worse? They seem like they've got worse. Or maybe they've always been like this and it was just my naivety as a kid. I just don't know wh-"

"Rob, calm down."

Jeff sits up and consoles Roberta, who takes deep breaths in and out to prevent herself from having a panic attack, something she hasn't had in years. She's learned to control them.

"Babe, I think you need to ring the social."

Roberta groans and sits up in bed. She knew that was coming. There's no way of talking to Jeff about it without him always reiterating back to the social.

"Jeff, you don't understand what it's like."

"And I can't begin to imagine, Rob. But, somehow, I feel like it's for the best. You have to think of how it's affecting Lydia in the long run. You might have not warmed to it, but maybe she'll find a lovely family if she goes into foster care. At the end of the day, she's not our kid."

Roberta makes a grunting noise and turns to face the wall with her back to Jeff. He'll never understand… But she hates to admit that he's right

"I'll sleep on it."

CHAPTER 43:

As he slowly fights to untangle the old ties inside his top dresser drawer, one by one they produce every colour except the one he's looking for.

"Hon, have you seen my black tie?"

"Not since you wore it to Betsy and Henry's wedding before Christmas."

"Hmmm," Dawson mumbles, before padding over to the wardrobe in his bare feet. Surely enough, inside his suit bag and hung loosely around his old shirt, he finds the culprit.

"Thanks, Hel. Found it."

Standing in front of the mirror and making himself look presentable, Dawson sighs at the thought of the oncoming day. Jill's funeral. The service is in the church near the park and then the community centre has been rented out for mourners to go and pay their respects, as well as scoff their faces with free tea and sandwiches. Dawson hopes that a familiar but unexpected face will turn up to help them with the case. God knows it needs a shove in the right direction, he thinks as he lifts his vibrating phone from the side table.

"Simpson, I'll be another five minutes."

"No, sir. I'm not outside. But I think you should hurry up anyway. It's Ward. He's finally come home."

CHAPTER 44:

Darren yanks out pieces of clothing and hastily shoves them in his bag as he rummages through his belongings. Not looking for anything in particular. Just enough to get by for another while. He glares at the alarm clock on his dresser. Just shy of 1pm. Everyone will be on their way to the funeral by now. He should be able to slip in and out of town undetected as long as he sticks to the routes he's already pre-planned. Pulling out his underwear drawer with such aggression, it comes loose and falls to the floor.

"Fuck!" he curses, scooping up a dozen pairs and driving them into the already overpacked bag.

He needs to be quick. He doesn't think they're watching the house, but he got out of the taxi two streets away and approached with caution anyway. With no signs of life, he had jogged around neighbouring houses before hopping his own low fence. The back door had made a loud clunk as it bounced off the wall, but he was too preoccupied with getting his shit together to notice. How had his life come to this? On the run from the police at the ripe young age of 23.

He had been in Glasgow on a stag do all weekend and arranged to see his friend, Jim, in Dumfries, before making the commute back to Rong Valley on Monday night. He was just sitting down to his second pint with Jim when his grandma had rung him.

"Darren, where are ya?"

"Still in Scotland, Nan. It's okay, the bins go out on Wednesday, not today."

"I'm not ringing about the bins you tosser. I may be old, but I'm not senile. Well… Not yet, anyway. Look, I've just had the police at my door. The girl next door, Jill Yates, she was found dead in the alleyway behind my house this morning."

He hadn't believed his ears. He brought the phone away and stared at it in disbelief, a look of confusion on his face. Had he really heard her right? He smiled and nodded at Jim, who was giving him a worried look, before stepping outside to hear better.

"What the hell are you talking about, Nan?"

"Young copper called Simpson has just paid me a visit. Asking me if I knew anything about the family. They seemed interested in you when they found out that it's *you* who takes my bins out."

"But... But... I haven't done anything. I've been in Scotland since Friday morning for Christ's sake."

"I know that, Dumbo. But they don't."

"Why didn't you tell them?"

"And what? Get them even more interested in you? Convenient that you skip the country as soon as my next door neighbour kicks the bucket. Murder investigation, she called it. If I were you, I'd stay away from here as long as you can."

"But I didn't do anything."

"They find out things, Darren. They'll find out what you did and that doesn't look good."

"But noth-"

"Ssh, don't say another word. They could be tapping my phone or God knows what else. Just stay clear, you hear me?"

"Yes, Nan."

And without a goodbye, the line went dead as his grandma hung up on him. He had returned to his seat in the pub and told Jim a made-up story about his nan going a bit mad. Seeing things. Luckily, Darren was able to get enough whiskeys down Jim's gullet to convince him to stay at the bar for a few more. *'Round 4'* he had called it, introducing a tray of Jägerbombs. Before long, the pair were so drunk that Jim had wrapped his arm around Darren, begging him to stay for the night.

"Fuck work tomorrow, I'll phone in sick," Jim had clinked glasses with his old friend, oblivious that his lightbulb spur-of-the-moment idea had been planted in his head by Darren hours before.

Jim's wife wasn't happy when the two landed home at 3am, singing U2's *'Vertigo'* which was bad enough on the karaoke with background music in the bar, so was disastrous echoing along Jim's lonely street.

"Look at the state of the pair of yees," his wife, Wanda, had hissed at them as they both lay in the tiny porch between the front door and the hallway, tangled amongst themselves and howling with laughter. "You're going to wake the whole bleedin' street."

And with that, she attempted to slam the hallway door shut, but it bounced off Darren's head, which brought a fresh rush of giggles from the two.

CHAPTER 45:

Wanda's mood didn't lighten the next day, as she marched out of the house and to work, leaving Darren and Jim slumped on the sofa with their heads fit to burst with pain. After an unsettled breakfast, Darren had convinced Jim to join him in the pub for a *'liquid lunch.'*

"I don't know, Daz," Jim had moaned. "It's really early and I'm still not feeling the best from last night's antics."

"Oh, come on. You had fun, didn't you?" Darren shouldered Jim, who was still feeling so delicate he almost toppled off the sofa.

"Wanda's really pissed."

"She will never know. Come on. One pint."

"Fine, fine".

Of course, Darren knew that one pint never meant just one pint. Especially not for Jim. He had grown up with the guy, before he moved to Scotland when he met Wanda at university. He knew he had a drinking problem. He was functional, but he would never say no to another. Shortly after 6pm, Jim had trudged off to the toilets and Darren had seen Wanda trying to ring, Jim's phone vibrating on the table ferociously. With a cough and a look around, Darren pocketed the phone and took a sip of his drink with feigned innocence.

Somewhere between the last beer and the tequila shot, Jim insisted on going home. Darren followed him, pointing out new pubs they hadn't tried yet, but they were futile attempts. It seemed Wanda had Jim's balls in a vice, too tight for his old pal to truly be himself. When they arrived home, it looked like flames were going to blow from Wanda's nostrils.

"What time's your train, Darren?" she asked, a strained smile on her face, eyes engulfing her head.

"Erm…" he faked checking his watch. "I think I've just missed the last one."

"That's too bad," she cooed, grabbing Jim by the cuff of his shirt and trying desperately to drag him inside.

"Now, c'mon, Wanda. We can't let him – sleep on the street," Jim hiccupped. After major convincing, Darren had made it through the threshold, but Wanda had stormed upstairs. Jim struggled to make Darren a bed out of old pillows and cushions, with the blanket reserved for the back of the armchair sprawled across the leather of the sofa.

"I'll sleep anywhere mate, you know me," Darren giggled.

Jim chuckled back and then bit his lip, staring at the blank TV screen.

"You alright, mate?"

"Yeah, yeah. Fine... It's just... Maybe you've overstayed your welcome a bit. Not with me. Of course not with me. It's been so good to catch up with you properly after all these years... But maybe with Wanda. I know she seems a nag... But she knows me, you know? She helped me through a lot, and I love her. When I met her... I was drinking every day. I barely went to class unless I had at least four beers in me. She just doesn't want me to go back down that path again. Maybe you should leave tomorrow. But we'll definitely make an effort to see each other more often. I'll make sure of it. Is that okay, mate?"

Darren had lay in the living room that night and heard the argument going on in the room above his head. It seemed to go on for hours. Despite their hushed tones, he had heard almost every word. His nan had rung earlier that day to say that she would keep him updated, but let it slip that they had returned to ask where he was.

BRADD CHAMBERS

Thankfully, she had said she didn't know. His mum and dad were still living the life of luxury on their cruise along the Mediterranean, so there was no chance of them getting contacted, not that they would know where he was regardless.

CHAPTER 46:

The following day, Darren had thought quick on his feet after getting dropped off at the station and waving goodbye to Jim. Less than an hour later, he was off the train at Carlisle and rolling into the local primary school that he knew Jack worked at. Marching through the school, he smiled and waved at the caretaker, trying to look as casual as possible. Like he belonged. He peered into every classroom until, somewhere on the second floor, he saw Jack's arm circling an equation on the chalkboard, addressing a bored looking class. Not wanting to knock and draw unwanted attention to himself, Darren poked his face against the window and waved. He distracted Jack long enough for him to do a double take, his mouth opened slightly. He mimed to his students and shut the door quietly behind him.

"Darren, what the hell are you doing here?"

"That's not a very nice way to greet your pal. Haven't seen you in ages, Jacky."

Darren pulled Jack into a hug, who patted his back cautiously in return.

179

"Erm… I saw you on Saturday night, Darren."

"You did? You did! Oh, well I haven't been home yet," he giggled.

Jack's eyes widened even more.

"You what?"

"Yeah, remember Jim? From school? Jim Brooks?"

Darren ignored Jack's glum face of unrecognition.

"Well, I was staying with him. Went on a few benders, you know?"

Darren pretended to glug an imaginary bottle in his hands before erupting into a roar of laughter. Jack looked up and down the corridor, blinking furiously.

"That's all well and good, mate. But why are you here?"

"Well, I was getting the train home and I saw that we were passing through Carlisle. I thought – you know what? I haven't been there before. Let's go see how my old buddy Jack is doing."

Jack's lips parted in an awkward smile.

"Erm… You know how I'm doing, Darren. You asked me on Saturday, remember?"

"Yeah, yeah. I know that. But we never got to really sit down and chat, you know?"

"I don't know what to say. Before Saturday, I hadn't seen you since before we left school. The only reason you knew I worked here is because I told you on Saturday. That was the length of the conversation we had."

"I know, but so many friends, so little time. How about a pint?"

"It's 10 o'clock in the morning, Darren. I'm teaching."

"At three, then?"

Jack rubbed the stubble on his chin.

"Fine. There's a pub down the street. The Queen's Gown, it's called. I'll meet you there at say... Four o'clock?"

"It's a date."

CHAPTER 47:

Jack looked surprised to see Darren when he trotted into the pub shortly before five.

"What took you so long, slow coach?"

"Sorry, I got caught up with marking. I didn't think you would've waited."

"Trying to avoid me, are ya?"

"No, no. Of course not," Jack went red in the face with embarrassment.

Darren laughed it off and slapped him on the back, making him drop one of his student's books, wrapped in its signature parcel paper, from his armful of files.

"Take a load off," Darren said, pulling up a chair from a neighbouring table.

Three hours, two burgers and a dozen pints later, the lads were more than reacquainted with each other.

"So, Daz," Jack slammed down his pint and wiped his mouth with the back of his hand, widening his eyes at the surprise of calling Darren by the nickname that everyone else, excluding

Jack, had called him back at RV High. "What's made you want to speak to me now?"

"What do you mean, mate?"

"You know we barely spoke in school," Jack slabbered, emboldened by the drink. "Why the sudden interest?"

Darren continued to circle the rim of his pint with his finger, before sucking the froth residue. Deep in thought and hoping for an excuse to pop into his head. Thankfully, one came.

"I felt bad, you know? Out of all the lads, we never spent any time together. I'm not running back to anything or anyone at home, so I thought I may as well take my time."

Jack nodded and smiled.

"Fair point."

When last orders were called, Jack had thrust his watch to his face.

"Shit! I have to get home."

Loose papers floated lazily through the air as Jack fought to gather everything with the initial hurried pace and the added effect of the alcohol. Darren stooped down to collect a few.

"Here, let me help ya. Do you live far from here?"

"No, no. Just a few streets away."

Dayna, Jack's girlfriend, couldn't have been a further cry from Wanda. Initially anyway. She welcomed Darren in with open arms and got to work on making tea and toast for the tipsy men.

"Jack, I couldn't stay here, could I? It's just... I doubt there's any more trains at this hour."

"Yeah, yeah. Say no more. We have a spare room. I'll just run it by Dayna."

Darren had smiled and plonked himself on the sofa in front of the TV, fully ready to make himself at home. After a few minutes, he heard a heated discussion coming from the door into the kitchen. Frowning, he stood and crossed the mat towards the source of the argument, his ear pressed against the door.

"You really don't know why he has just come out of the blue?"

"I don't know, Dayna... But I don't think he has it in him. He's sound."

"Sound? You were going on about how much of a tool he was all weekend when you got home."

"I know, but after sitting with him tonight... I don't know. He seems different."

"Yeah, 'cause you're drunk. Drunk on alcohol and the lies that he's fed you."

"You were fine with him thirty seconds ago?"

"Yeah, I was. But that was before you told me who he was. I thought he was a teaching friend or someone from around these parts. Not one of your scummy mates from Rong Valley."

There was a silence as she presumably composed herself, clearly distraught at having upset Jack. Darren imagined him getting taken aback, perhaps even retreating a few steps.

"I'm sorry. That was too far... Look, I don't know why he's targeting you, Jack. But I need you to wake up tomorrow, sober and in the cold light of day and think about the mistake that you're about to make. That little kiddie was killed, it's all over the news, and he hasn't been home. Do you really think that this is unrelated? I want him out, J. *Out!*"

Safe to say that Darren had known when he wasn't welcome. He'd trotted out of there before Jack had time to make up a sorry excuse. What had he been thinking anyway? Jack and Darren had said the bare minimum to each other all through high school. Within the group of five lads, they never met up or associated with each other individually. How did he think he could trust him? Admitting defeat, Darren had drunkenly made his way to the train station and,

185

embarrassingly, fell asleep on one of the hard, plastic chairs. When the first available train travelling south was called this morning, he had boarded it.

CHAPTER 48:

Continuing to throw as much of his miserable life as he can into an overnight bag, Darren retreats to the kitchen to see if there's any food that can be savoured. Halfway through picking through the tins of soups and tuna, he freezes as there's a knock on the back door. He knows it was left open. He knows there's someone right behind him. And, although crouched down at the bottom cabinet, there's no hope of his guest missing him.

Slowly, he stands and turns towards the intruder. There, in his sharp black suit, stands DI Dawson. Darren recognises him instantly. His bald head had greeted every pub telly screen he'd been in over the past few days. He coughs and steps over the threshold.

"Mr Ward?"

"Yes?"

"I'm Detective Inspector Donald Dawson. I'm here to ask you a few questions."

CHAPTER 49:

Simpson's radio crackles to life, but the message is lost in transmission. Dawson sounds stressed. She brings it from her belt and hovers it over her mouth.

"Sorry, sir. Could you rep-"

The rest of her response is cut short as the front door of Darren Ward's house flies open, the edge of the cheap plastic colliding sharply with Simpson's head, making her topple backwards. Tripping over the flower pot, she finds herself spread-eagled, face down on the grass. As she raises her head sharply, she sees the feet of, who she can only presume to be Ward, sprinting away.

"Bratton, Headley, McKay, subject has escaped through the front door, now making his way west down Meneen's Street on foot," she barks into the radio, still in her outstretched hand.

She climbs to her knees and presses her hand against the pounding in her head, feeling the blood trickle down her fingers. Her eyes closed, wincing against the pain.

"I don't get paid enough for this," she whimpers.

She feels the thunder of movement around her, the officers surrounding the house tearing off after Ward. Footsteps at the front door indicates that Dawson has now vacated the house.

"Simpson, are you okay?"

"Fine, now get after him," she brandishes her pointing finger blindly in the wrong direction.

Dawson hesitates, then joins the pursuit, panting into his radio that medical assistance is required.

CHAPTER 50:

Thankfully, despite knowing the area significantly better than the officers, Ward was arrested within minutes.

"Why were you running?" Dawson growls at him, sitting opposite the detectives in Interview Room 1, his lawyer by his side.

"No comment."

"It does make it look a bit suspicious, don't you think?"

"No comment."

Dawson's blood starts to boil.

"Where were you on the night of Sunday March 18th and the early hours of Monday March 19th, Mr Ward?" he repeats for the third time.

Dawson thinks he's cracked him as he opens his mouth slightly, but to no avail.

"No comment."

Dawson slams his fist on the stop button of the recorder and storms out of the room, Simpson in tow.

"If I was prime minister the '*no comment*' plea would be banned," Dawson grunts, striding down the corridor at full speed, leaving Simpson to half-jog in his wake.

"Sir?"

"Not now," he waves his hands at whoever approached him, not even taking time to register their face.

Barrelling into the incident room, Dawson and Simpson spread the reports of the case and the information from Ward's file over the huge table.

"So... The only thing we've done this rat in for is this drunken fight?"

"Yeah, boss," Simpson finds the relevant sheet. "He was arrested in 2004 for fighting outside Spoons on Chessington Street. Nothing serious, we just kept him and the other party overnight, but neither of them pressed any charges."

"There has to be something else," Dawson spits, eyes flicking from sheet to sheet, looking for any sort of key word to jump out and wave at him.

A knock on the door makes Dawson sigh heavily.

"Sorry to interrupt, detectives."

It's the young boy who brought them the Dylan Gardener case a few days ago.

"Yes, Smit. What's up?" Simpson has her bandaged head resting on her hand, gazing at the officer with a bored expression on her face.

"DS Simpson… Your head. Are you-"

"I'm fine, Smit. Please…"

"Oh, okay. Erm… I've just been thinking… Well…"

"Spit it out son," Dawson spins around and glares at the boy.

"Right… Sorry. Well… After taking a further look into Gardener, I decided maybe it'd be a good idea to study the entire register. You know… Just in case. There are two people within a ten-mile radius of the town on there. One being our friend Dylan Gardener, obviously, and the second, a Mr Tobias Hegarty. He's coming into his seventies now, but he was approached regardless. He was at a game of poker with some of his friends on the night in question. Don't worry, his alibis have been checked," he extends his finger to Dawson, who has puffed out his chest, ready to intrude into the findings.

Defeated, Dawson nods his head for consented continuation.

"So, that was a bit short lived. However, I scanned back to see if anyone had recently moved out of the area. Again, it's not much of a list. Only one name arose, a Mr Shane Miller. He was arrested some years ago for having indecent images of young boys on his computer. He has since moved to Brighton after his release to start afresh. But guess where his last known address in Rong Valley was?"

He stands triumphant, but Dawson still stares at him, waiting for an answer. When none come, he opens his mouth to ask the boy why he's wasting their time, but he's interrupted by an outburst from Simpson beside him.

"50 Connolly's Estate!"

CHAPTER 51:

The community centre is filled with the muffled sounds of hushed conversations. People too scared to speak out of term or speak too loudly in case they offend a member of the family or a fellow mourner. The service was beautiful, with the minister knowing Jill well. She helped out at the local youth clubs when she could. With the growing numbers of ASBOs in young people around Promised Hill, the minister and church have begun to work closely with the clubs to alter people's minds and keep them occupied and off the streets.

Roberta is perched on one of the rickety stools carelessly spread around the hall to accommodate the stampede of people who turned up. She has her Dictaphone resting in her blazer pocket, protruding out just a smidge to catch the snippets of conversation she's having with people without giving away its presence. She's just finished speaking with Jill's English teacher, who had nothing but good words to say, when she spots Donna Yates floating around by the sandwiches. As she smiles her goodbye to the teacher, she starts over towards the grieving mother, her arm rested against her side in such a way that the microphone of her recorder is angled directly in front of her.

"Mrs Yates, hi."

Donna jumps as if she had been snuck up on. When she sees it's Roberta, she looks back down at the food before mumbling a greeting.

"I was wondering if you had a moment to talk?"

Donna looks around before nodding discreetly.

"How about outside? Bit noisy in here, ain't it? And we won't be interrupted," Roberta smiles before linking arms with the woman and leading her outside.

They rest against the low graffitied wall at the entrance of the community centre and gaze out at the rows of houses spread out in front of them. Promised Hill Community Centre is almost at the very top of the incline, so most of the town can be seen from where they're standing.

"It's very relaxing up here, isn't it?"

Donna nods her head.

"Mrs Yates... Can I call you Donna?"

She shrugs and starts sucking her fingers.

195

"Donna… I would love to hear about what happened that night. From your own point of view. Have you seen the service that this town has provided for Jill? They're all behind you. One hundred percent. Your exclusive will continue to get more people behind you. They're sad today. If we can get an article in tomorrow's paper, with your story, of course, that sadness can be turned to anger. We *will* find her killer, Donna. You can trust me."

Tears have sprung up in Donna's eyes and she looks longingly at Roberta before sniffing and allowing them to slide down her cheeks.

"You don't understand…"

"Help me understand, Donna."

"Where was my invite to this pity party?"

Both woman jump at the booming voice behind them, making the hairs on Roberta's neck ping up immediately. She spins around to see Kane on the other side of the wall, breathing in a long drag of his cigarette and letting it swirl around his lungs for a substantial amount of time, before exhaling it right in the reporter's face.

"C'mon, Donna. Clara is getting restless. It's time to go."

Almost as if a surge of electricity has run through her, Donna's up on her feet and skirting around the wall within seconds. As Roberta watches her trudge towards the carpark, Kane leans in until she can see the cuts on his freshly shaved chin.

"This is your last warning. Stay the fuck away from my family."

The pair don't break eye contact until Kane smirks, spits on the ground centimetres from Roberta's shoes and turns to follow his wife. Roberta shivers and, when Kane is a safe distance in front of her, swivels her legs over the wall and starts back towards the community centre. As she nears the hall, she can't help but notice, from the corner of her eye, three burly men staring at her. But when she turns her head in their direction they all have their heads together, deep in discussion, before leading off down towards the car park and away from the scared journalist.

CHAPTER 52:

The phone blares out, cutting the tension in Dawson's office. Its ring echoes around in his head before he reluctantly reaches for the receiver.

"DI Dawson."

"Hi, Dawson. It's Henderson."

DS Henderson from Plymouth Police had agreed to check out Shane Miller after their phone call yesterday. It took all of Dawson's energy not to drive down to Brighton himself, but the 11-hour trip there and back discouraged him. He knew his resources were needed in Rong Valley. Not to mention the press would have a field day if they heard he'd flown the nest, and they still had Darren Ward in custody... For now, anyway.

"Henderson, any luck?"

"I'm afraid not, sir. I went to see Miller last night and he hasn't returned to Rong Valley since he was released. He hasn't even left Brighton in the few months he's been here. He's too frightened. Apparently, a few gangs heard what he was in for when he was in prison. He had a few lucky escapes, but they vowed that they knew people on the outside. That they would make him suffer for what he did. Scared for his own safety, that's why he fled all the way down here."

Dawson's jaw is clenched.

"Well... Just because he said he hasn't returned doesn't mean that it's true?"

"That may be so, sir. But he told me he was working the graveyard shift at the local factory, Naran and Wells, last Sunday night."

"And when did he clock out?"

"6:04am, sir."

Dawson curses under his breath. For a standard eight-hour shift, Miller would've had to be at the factory for 10pm at the latest. Take away the five-and-a-half-hour trip from Rong Valley to Brighton, ignoring traffic, he would've had to have left here by 4:30pm. Donna told Simpson she last saw Jill after 7pm. The math doesn't add up.

"Fine, not what I'd hoped for, but thanks for chasing this up. I presume Naran and Wells have security footage?"

"They do, sir."

"Can I get a copy?"

"I'll contact them and ask for it to be sent over right away."

"Thanks, Henderson."

Dawson slams down the phone and rubs his tired eyes with his hands. It had been a long night trying to get Ward to say anything other than '*no comment*.' In the end, they left him to stew in the cells overnight. Hopefully, this morning, he'll be a bit more cooperative. Approaching Interview Room 1 with the intentions of ripping this lad apart, Dawson and Simpson are side-tracked, called over to DC Austin's desk.

"We've just had Cherrie Cooke on the phone," he stares up at the detectives.

"And what of it?" Dawson sniffs.

"Seems Ward has been in contact with her. She says she's got something to say. But she wouldn't speak to me. She wants you," he nods his head towards Simpson.

CHAPTER 53:

"The boy's an absolute melon," Cherrie offers the detectives a cigarette, "but he's no bloomin' murderer."

"How can you be so sure?" Dawson narrows his eyes at the elderly lady.

"'cause I know him," Cherrie eyes him suspiciously. "God knows his mother never gave a shit. Always unloaded him off to me when she got the chance. And let's not start on his father."

The grandfather clock's ticking in the hall of the tiny house is all that can be heard as Cherrie flicks the lighter and breathes in hungrily.

"Well if that's the case then where has he been all this time, and why did he run when we approached him?" Dawson asks.

"It's a long story," Cherrie mumbles, her eyes transfixed on a damp spot on her ceiling.

"We have all the time in the world," Simpson sits forward.

Seeming to trust Simpson, as if Dawson can't hear what she says if the conversation is angled towards her, Cherrie slides her narrow behind inches further until it threatens to topple off the chair.

"The boy was in Scotland up until yesterday, then he stayed with friends in Carlisle. Don't ask me their names, he'll be able to tell you. I'm sure you can ring your mates up there and ask for CCTV and all that jazz."

Simpson and Dawson weren't suspecting this. There's so many questions that Dawson wants to ask, but now that Simpson's earned Cherrie's trust, he doesn't want to go shattering it. He glares at Simpson, silently willing for her to snap out of the trance as she sits calculating the old lady's recent admission.

"Okay…"

"He didn't come home 'cause I told him not to."

The detectives look startled again.

"He was coming home on Monday night, but then you called in earlier that day and I told him to take his time. I hoped that you'd find the killer by the time he made it home and he wouldn't have to get dragged through this. He's went through enough shit as it is."

"You do know you lied to the police, perverting the course of ju-"

Dawson is cut short with a wave of Simpson's hand as Cherrie's head physically retreats back a few inches from his input.

"Why did you lie, Cherrie?" Simpson almost sounds sympathetic.

"'cause I didn't want him to be put in jail."

"But if you're so sure that he didn't do it… Then what was the problem?"

Cherrie has been speaking so much that her cigarette has nearly burnt out without the help of her lungs. She quickly stubs it out and reaches for another, her hands shaking slightly, whether from nerves or old age is indistinct. When she's had a few drags of her fresh one, she looks back at Simpson, tapping her foot nervously.

"I had to tell the lad off before Christmas."

The detectives lean forward, but Cherrie isn't offering anymore information without prompt.

"Why, Cherrie?"

"He had a car for a while. His mate Arnold went to visit his family in Spain and didn't want to leave his car unattended for nearly two weeks around these parts, I'm sure you understand."

The two detectives nod their heads, reminiscing privately about all the times they've had to attend the scene where a car was burnt out or stolen, or stolen and then burnt out.

"Anyway, he thought he was this big shot. Driving around the town until all hours of the morning. Trying to pick up drunk girls and showing off to his mates. Boys will be boys," she gives a gummy grin. "But one day when he was coming over here, I saw from this window-"

She points at the narrow window right beside her chair, overlooking the street.

"-that he was moving very slowly up the road towards me. I was thinking he was drinking or he had wrecked the car or whatever. So many things went through my head. But then I saw the Yates girl… "

"Jill?"

"Yeah, Jill. She was coming home and hiding her face from his car, walking as fast as she could. He was chatting her up and what not. When he parked up and came into the house, I gave him a good slap. Told him he was a perv and the girl was only 15. He said he didn't know. To be fair, he had never seen her before and her school uniform was buried under so many layers to hide from the cold. He hasn't seen her since. I made sure of that. The look of disgust on his face was obvious when he found out he was trying to get off with a school girl. But you know you lot-"

She brandishes her cigarette-holding-hand at the detectives, causing a circle of smoke to paint an obstruction between them.

"-you see it all the time. On The Bill and Midsummer Murders and all them other programmes. You hear of something like this and you latch onto it. I didn't want him to be put away for something he hasn't done. He's not the full shilling, you know? But he's not capable of something like this."

Visibly exhausted, she returns her back to the welcoming groove of her chair and sucks the last breaths of nicotine from her dying cigarette.

CHAPTER 54:

The sun splits the sky in anomalous April style. Some days it could be close to snowing. Others, like summer come early, tricking people into the false pretence that they can leave the house without a jacket.

Dawson rests on the bench out his back garden after bringing his lunch home. Too embarrassed by the continuing spite of hatred from the press. Not wanting to show his face in the lunch room at the station when it's already plastered on several newspapers strewn across the coffee stained table top.

He thinks about the last few weeks as he munches into his wife's carefully made sandwich, still crust-free after all these years. Darren Ward had finally admitted his whereabouts, and his cronies in Scotland, as well as CCTV footage from everywhere he had been that weekend, confirmed his alibis. Shane Miller wasn't bothered again, but Dawson watched and re-watched the footage sent from his factory regardless. Itching to find some loop hole. Apart from a teenage boy from RV high who thought it would be funny to tell his mother that *he* killed Jill as an April Fool's joke, the case had basically run dry. Lost steam. The Super had taken all extra hands off the case, and was almost close to calling it quits altogether. She mentally castrated Dawson every time she rang to find that no progress was made. No new evidence. No new lead. Just reiterating the same thing she'd heard since day one. Dawson had even contemplated putting forward a request to dig up Jill's body to give the coroner another look, but decided against it. He was getting enough of a lashing.

He stares at a premature bee, circulating the budded flowers on Helen's patch. What is the killer doing now? How is he so skilled? Was it by chance or was it a calculated attack? Someone they know? Someone they doubt? Or someone completely new? Someone who fled the scene and is now miles and miles away, lapping it up in the sun and laughing over a cocktail, boasting about committing the perfect murder.

"Dad?"

Dawson spurts out his juice and bangs his chest to stop himself from choking.

"Alicia," he says, spinning around, tears streaming, "you scared the shit out of me."

"Sorry. What are you doing here?"

"I – I – Uhh... I forgot my lunch. Then thought it was such a beautiful day, I... Hey, never mind about me. What are *you* doing home?"

Alicia looks away and pushes her hair behind her ear, a nervous tick she's had since she was in nappies.

"We have PE last period after lunch. I'm not really feeling up to running about, so I came home instead."

"Leesh, you shouldn't be walking about on your own. Espec-"

"Dad, I'm almost 16. I'm sure I can walk home from school in broad daylight."

Dawson returns to his chocolate bar and mumbles a despondent agreement. Alicia purses her lips and marches inside, pulls something unhealthy looking from the fridge and disappears. Dawson sighs. She hasn't been the same since that night with Carl. He can't enquire too much as she'll figure out he may have something to do with it. From what he's heard from Helen, Carl left the house without a goodbye and hasn't answered any of her calls or texts. Good, he thinks to himself, staring off into the garden again. However, he can't stop but feel a small twinge of guilt at being the reason for his daughter's unhappiness. His thought process is interrupted by the blare of his phone.

"Simpson?"

"Sir, where are you? I can't find you anywhere."

"I'm at home, Simpson. I came home for lunc-"

"Never worry about that now. Quick. We need you at the top of Promised Hill. It's Donna Yates. I think she's going to jump."

CHAPTER 55:

Tears sting at Donna's eyes as she stands at the edge of the precipice, gazing down at the jagged-out rocks and rusty bushes sure to tear her apart on her way down the escarpment. Although the spurious valley is hidden from the harsh weather, being at the top of Promised Hill brings the north's bitter sting of wind. It slaps off her face and brings back memories of Kane. How it started. Her heavily pregnant with Jill. *Jill!*

Finally, all the tension built up inside her over the weeks rips out of her. The wind carries her screams as she curses everything and everyone. She shouts at the landmarks that she's grown to detest in this dead-end town. She shouts at the bastards who kept her here and made her feel the way she feels today. But, more than anything, she shouts at herself. Cursing her ignorance and naivety for dropping out of school and marrying Kane so young. Thinking he would change. He convinced her that everything would be okay if they lived together, if they got married, if she stopped seeing her friends so wouldn't have to listen to their protests and concerns about their distrust in him.

She always had an inkling that it would end like this. Ever since she was a teenager. She wants back control of her life again. And the only way to do that is to end it. On her own terms. Her throat feels blistered as she stops screaming. She takes one step forward and feels the fragility of the earth this close to the edge. She can see the grass moving, and feels the ground unearthing beneath her. She just needs to add more pressure.

"Donna!"

The wind that carried her screams are now carrying something else. She strains to hear, thinking she's imagining it. Then, from the corner of her eye she sees fluorescent yellow. Turning, she's shocked to see three police officers surrounding DI Dawson and DS Simpson, all approaching cautiously. Her knees buckle and she almost topples over. She falls on her bum and ignores the threatening ground below her left foot. The last thing she sees are pebbles and bits of earth falling into the abyss beneath before arms surround her.

CHAPTER 56:

The tea in the polystyrene cup swish-swashes with the shakes of Donna's hand, until half of it is spilled all over the table of Interview Room 2.

Dawson and Simpson stare across at her. The tape had begun recording about five minutes ago. She still hasn't said a word. But neither of the detectives probe her. *She* had wanted to talk. *She* had answers. And with the current state of the case, they would happily welcome some.

Donna glances up at the duo, before reverting her eyes back to the spilled tea, taking her hands away from the cup before she makes more of a mess. She finds it difficult to interlock her fingers, but when she does, she places them delicately on her scruffy jeans. She murmurs something so discreet that even the silence in the tiny room doesn't echo it.

"I'm sorry, Donna?"

"I couldn't stop him," she whispers, a bit louder for them to hear.

"You couldn't stop who, Donna?"

Her eyes fill with silent tears.

"It's not my fault."

"Please, Donna. Tell us what happened."

She sniffs and pulls a fist towards her lips, but it's too late. The flood gates have opened.

"I tried so hard to stop it. To stop him."

Moments later, when the fit of tears has subsided, she takes a sip of the cold tea.

"That night she died... Kane was in a horrible mood. Man City had lost in the footy. He was more drunk than usual. Drowning his sorrows probably. Came home in foul form. Started ranting and raving about the best years of his life down the shitter. Clara was still up. I'd told her to go to bed, but she was having none of it. Wanted to play a while longer. Jill tried too, but she was listening to no-one. Had found some rotten looking toy out on the street. A pony, from what I can remember.

"I knew both of them were usually in bed before he gets home. That's the best place for them. Especially when he's pissed. When he came into the living room, he gave both girls a look over, before staring at me. As if it was my job. Jill got off the sofa and tried to lift Clara, but she started throwing a tantrum. Giving up, she skirted past her father and up the stairs. He grunted and sat in his seat, turning the telly on. Clara was singing and giving the horse a stupid voice. I saw him glaring at her a few times."

Donna swallows before continuing.

"After a few minutes, he told her to shut up and get to bed. She stuck out her lip and climbed onto the sofa. She wrapped my coat around her and lay watching the telly too. He shouted at her to get upstairs again. She still didn't move. He started cursing and yelling, before lobbing the remote at her. Hit her square in the head. She started crying, which made things worse. He always hates her crying. That's when Jill came back down. Trying to coax her up the stairs again. When Clara wouldn't stop crying, he went for her. Jill screamed and pulled her off the sofa. He was so drunk he toppled over it. He was so mad. He went to grab for Clara, but Jill forced her up the stairs, shouting at her to go to bed. Jill kept shouting for him not to hurt Clara. He floored her with one punch. When he started kicking her, I saw blood all over my mat. That's when I screamed at him to stop. Tried to pull him away by his arm, but he turned and hit me a thump as well.

"After a while, she stopped crying and screaming, but he continued hitting her. Taking out all his frustration on her. When he grew tired, he fell back into his chair and lit a fag. It took a few moments for me to realise that she was dead. I roared at him. Calling him a murderer, but he grabbed and twisted my arm. I thought he might break it. He told me to wash the mat, and he disappeared with the body. When he came back, I was scrubbing the floors. There was no blood on it, but just in case. He scared the shit out of me.

"That night, in bed, he threatened me. Told me he'd kill me if I ever told anyone. I haven't slept in weeks. Just knowing what he's done. I thought someone else would tell, or you'd figure it out, you know, like on them cop shows on telly. But no one ever did. I've just been eaten up with guilt. In the early hours of this morning, I decided enough was enough. I let him have sex with me when he woke up this morning, and made him breakfast before he went to work. Just pretending everything was normal. And now I'm here, but I'm begging, please don't let me go back there. You hear about it all the time. New lives and identities. Please, help me. I'm petrified of what he might do."

"But…" Simpson's eyes have been unblinking, registering the new information. "…The neighbours. Wouldn't they have heard? I'm guessing this isn't the first time this aggression has surfaced."

"Oh, he's got everyone on that street wrapped around his finger," the first sign of anger blurts out of Donna behind her snotty nose. "If it's not drugs, it's alibis. If not that, then help with robbing something. They've all got his back. And if they don't... They're petrified of him. I wished someone would've came forward. I almost went around and begged them. But they were all too scared."

She breaks down again, her shoulders shaking, the last of her confidence and energy erupting out of her in one last wail. Simpson thanks her for her bravery and informs her of everything to expect in the coming months.

When the interview is terminated she's being shipped off to Woman's Aid, a secluded cottage out in the country for battered women and their children. They tell her that Clara will be brought to her as soon as they can take her out of school without suspicion, but she refuses her.

"I don't want anything to do with her. She's better off without me. Give her to someone else. Anything's better than a life on the run. Even our old life on Promised Hill."

CHAPTER 57:

"Bloody hooligans," Kane spits as he lights a cigarette and rests his head against the back wall of Dave's Bookies.

He couldn't give a rat's arse what age these boys coming in to gamble their pocket money away are. They're too stupid to look for patterns and anomalies. More money in the business', and therefore his own, pocket. But with the council threatening an audit, they'd shut the place down if they saw anyone underage. After refusing to serve them without ID, the lads threw all the slips on the floor and spat on the window before giving him their signature middle fingers. Little do they know that Kane knows all their fathers, very well. He sure won't be letting them away with this.

Speak of the devil, there's Matty ringing, probably looking to see if Kane knows anyone with any Charlie.

"Matty, mate I'm at work. Will have to-"

"Kane. Quick, you need to get out of town."

Kane frowns and glares at a piece of moss on the wall opposite him. Matty wouldn't mess around with stuff like this, and he's been his accomplice on many an operation. What's happened?"

"Matty... Can you speak?"

"Yeah, I can. I've just left the police station. Had me in overnight for fighting last night. Bastard deserved it. But that's neither here nor there. No Kane, I just saw your missus walking into the station with those two coppers that are all over the news. I think she might be about to fess up."

"Fess up to what exactly?"

"Just thought I'd give you a heads up. Just in case..."

The line then goes dead and Kane extends his phone in front of him and stares until the backlight goes off, reflecting his shocked face.

"That *cunt*!"

CHAPTER 58:

"And what's this, Clara?"

Mrs Cole bends over and examines Clara's art piece, thankful that the little girl doesn't smell today, and there are no visible lice in her hair. Of course, it isn't the child's fault. It all lies with the parents. She stares at the static red, orange and yellows throughout the piece.

"Is this fire?"

Clara nods, her tongue protruding from her lips in concentration, and digs her black crayon in harder until the paper threatens to rip. Mrs Cole blinks feverishly before giving a nervous laugh and crossing to another student.

Moments later, the sound of a hectic knock bounces around the room. Mrs Cole smiles at the children, all of their beady eyes on her for recognition, before crossing to the main door of the portacabin. She's greeted by a panting man, who has clearly run for the majority of his journey. Beads of sweat travel down from his mousey-brown hair and into his thick, greying beard. His eyes are wild and oddly familiar, and they penetrate into the teacher's, making her momentarily scared for the safety of her students, and herself.

"May I help you?"

"Daddy!"

She spins around to see Clara skipping over before giving her father a cautious hug. So, this is the famous Mr Yates. If only for his daughter being killed mere weeks ago, she would've loved to have sat down and discussed everything that's went on since September, both academically and personally, for the benefit of Clara of course.

"C'mon, Pumpkin."

Kane hoists Clara over his shoulders, much to the delight of his daughter who screams and frails her legs about playfully.

"I'm sorry, Mr Yates I presume?"

He grumbles his affirmation before barrelling out of the classroom.

"Excuse me, Mr Yates, but I'm afraid you can't-"

"She's my daughter."

Mrs Cole is now jogging to keep up with the bull of a man, who takes a short cut through the playground and the grass, despite the explicit sign asking for no-one to trod on it.

"That may be so, sir, but there are rules and regulation-"

"I've already sorted out all that crap."

"Mr Yates, please, I can't allow you t-"

"To take my own daughter? I'm sure I bloody well can."

"I'm sorry, but if you don't slow down and discuss what is going on I'm afraid I'll have to-"

She gasps as he turns around and doesn't shy away from having his face inches from her own. She steps back and swallows.

"Look, Mr Yates, I know that the past f-"

"If you really have to know, there's been a breakthrough in the case."

She looks at him shocked. She, of course, couldn't resist giving the front of the papers a mull over whilst waiting in the queue for her morning petrol station coffee. She's only human after all. Although she isn't into gossip and such, she's fully up-to-date in the goings on of the murder in this small town.

"A new lead?"

"Something like that. That's all I can tell you."

And without another word, Kane struts the last remaining steps to the staff carpark, before turning the corner towards the front exit, leaving Mrs Cole with a desire to join him, an urge to go straight to the office and report this incident and a duty of care to return to her remaining students.

221

CHAPTER 59:

Dawson and Simpson arrive at 52 Connolly's Estate and are met in the small front yard by DC Austin.

"He's nowhere to be seen sir, house has been checked top to bottom."

Dawson curses.

"I take it Dave's Bookies is the same?" Austin's head turns to the side.

"Yeah, I would say the bastard fled when he saw us approach, but we had men covering all sides."

"And there was no one else working with him?"

"No, we've tried to get in contact with David himself, but Donna's said that we shouldn't bother. Would rather spit on us before helping us apparently."

"So, what should we do now," Simpson waves innocently at Cherrie as she cranes her neck from her seat to get a better look at the disruption outside.

"Station someone down the street there," Dawson points towards the red bricked house five doors down, "we'll try the pubs. Hopefully he's went AWOL from work for a pint and not because he knows he's a wanted man."

CHAPTER 60:

The bastards were too quick for him. He'll give them that. No matter. He skirts around the corner and down Windsor Place, trying to drag Clara along as fast as he can without making a scene. Knocking on number 39, he's greeted with the '*ayyys*' of Mark.

"Yeah, yeah. Are you gonna let me in or what's the story?"

Stepping to the side, he lets Kane and his daughter through.

"Daddy, I have to wee."

Kane looks at Mark expectantly, who points to the open door at the end of the hall. Clara hurries along, hands covering her crotch, before clicking the door closed.

"So, to what do I owe the pleasure?" Mark lights a cigarette and flops down on his green sofa, placing his feet on his mum's old pouffe.

"I'm actually looking a favour, mate."

"Anything."

"I need out your back gate, through to the alley."

Mark squints and blows out the smoke, looking confused and suspicious.

"No questions."

Mark shrugs before groaning, pulling himself up and sliding into the kitchen. Bringing a rusty key similar to his own from the drawer, Mark hands it over to Kane before offering him a cigarette and a beer.

"No time," Kane scoops Clara up into his arms, her hands, still wet from the sink, around his neck.

In the alleyway, dimly lit by the sun hiding behind a worrying cloud, Clara starts to sense that something's wrong.

"This is where they found Jilly, Daddy."

"What? Where did you hear that?"

"In school... They told me she was dead.. Found here... I'm scared... I want Mummy."

"Well, Mummy's not here. So ssh now."

Clara starts to cry and Kane drops her down onto her bum, before brandishing his pointing finger in her face.

"Stop crying. Right now. You hear me?"

Of course, this makes her worse. She starts to sob uncontrollably and he kicks the wall in frustration, before cursing at his own stupidity, his toe throbbing from the collision.

"Now, look. I'm going to climb this wall and then open this gate for you to get in. Stay here, okay?"

Clara moans and shivers with the tears, before nodding sullenly. Kane jerks his head from left to right to try and find a suitable foothold. Anything to help him scale this wall. Eventually he gives up and tries to jump, striking one hand out to touch the top.

"Fuck!"

He falls to the ground and glares at his hand, now red with blood. Clasping his free hand over his injured one, he hops on one foot to see over the wall. Sure enough, jagged out of the concrete are dozens of pieces of broken glass. A deterrent for burglars. How the fuck had he forgotten about that?

CHAPTER 61:

Stepping out of The Rusty Crown and giving the road a good look up and down, Dawson groans as he's interrupted by his phone.

"Dawson."

"Hi, Mr D."

He freezes. Carl? How the hell did he get this number?

"Don't hang up."

Dawson's snarl intensifies.

"I've got information I think you might like."

It kills Dawson to think he's now hanging on Carl's every word.

"Go on."

"Kane Yates. With a little kiddie, think it's his daughter. Seen down around the corner from his house. Windsor Place."

"Seen by who?"

"Me."

Dawson curses and barks instructions down his radio before bringing the phone back up to his ear with a confused look.

"How did you know we're looking for him?"

"Word gets around fast around these parts, Mr D."

"Fine."

He knew it was coming, but he still gets enraged as Carl tries to arrange some form of a reward for his information, whether money or his daughter, he'll never know. Dawson hangs up before blocking Carl's number and hurrying to his car.

CHAPTER 62:

Cherrie has just finished washing her hands in the grubby, what once was cream-coloured, sink when she hears the bangs. Hobbling over to the ledge, she flicks the doily designed curtains back and peaks her head out of her bathroom window.

There, in the alley, lies the other Yates girl. Crying and hugging her arms, seemingly staring at whatever's in front, but because of the position of her own rear yard, and the Yates' next door, she can't see what's happening. The bangs seem to be coming from the other side of the Yates' back gate, and she watches as it vibrates with impact. A few blows later, the wood cracks nearer the bottom, and the next few hits make the wood split the entire way up. Pushing an arm through the gap and twisting the key, the door propels forward to reveal Kane standing, blood gushing from one hand and murder in his eyes.

Cherrie gasps and retreats back from view, before climbing down the stairs as fast as she can, which in her current physical condition, isn't very quick. When she reaches the phone in the hall, she asks the operator to put her through to DS Simpson right away.

CHAPTER 63:

"Daddy? Daddy? Daddy?" Clara wails, following her father around the house, arms by her side and tears and snot pouring from her face, currently scrunched up in fear.

Kane thunders up the stairs and struggles to lift the latch to the roof space. Once manoeuvred, he winces with pain as his injured hand grasps around in the dusty darkness, before finally landing on their suitcase.

"Daddy? Daddy? Daddy?"

Pulling the case down, he heaves open his wardrobe and throws a few necessary items into it. Grabbing the mountain of empty, detouring shoeboxes and pulling them to the ground, he finds the red one he's looking for. Opening the lid, he pours the containment of money, substances and fake passports into the case.

"Daddy? Daddy? Daddy?"

Once that's done, he reaches for his phone and searches for Scumpy's number.

"Scumpy, I need you to meet me at the train station. Right away."

"Daddy? Daddy? Daddy?"

"What do you need, mate?"

"Tickets. Anywhere. Preferably to an airport."

"Daddy? Daddy? Daddy?"

Silence follows on the line, he can faintly hear the sound of a keyboard.

"Gatwick alright?"

"Yeah, great. Thanks, pal."

Chucking his phone into the case, satisfied with hearing the plonk as it hits the clothes, he zips it up and lets it slide down the stairs, coming to a stop just short of the front door, before tumbling down after it.

"Daddy? Daddy? Daddy?"

He throws the kitchen cabinet's door open so aggressively that one of the hinges comes off. Grabbing a few bottles and tucking them under his arm, he scavenges the rest of the room for more supplies.

"Daddy? Daddy? Daddy"

"What?" he roars, spinning around and grabbing his daughter's head with his free hand and dragging it down to the floor. She squeals in pain.

"What do you want? What the fuck do you want?" he starts shaking her, but she cries on. "Shut up! Shut the fuck up!"

His eyes revert down to her smooth, innocent neck and he wraps both huge hands around her throat, dropping the bottles clumsily to the floor. Finally, she's silenced. Her eyes bulge and she gazes up at her father with a fear he's never seen on her face before. She chokes and splutters. Still he drives on.

Moments later, a loud bang is heard at the front door. Scrabbling off his daughter, Kane lurches forward and flies out of the back door, through the alley and snaps Mark's gate closed before he hears the police making their presence known in his own house. Sod Clara, she was a hinderance and was to be used as a distraction. He'll have to make the journey alone.

CHAPTER 64:

The howls echo along the packed street as Clara is shipped into a social worker's car with promises that they surely can't keep. Dawson sits on the low wall outside the Yates' house and stares at the flashing blue beacons, now silenced but the ringing of the sirens still fresh in his mind. They had almost caught the bastard. And just in time it seems. Any longer and the girl could've been seriously hurt... Or worse.

Uniforms are returning from their door-to-door questioning from the surrounding streets, but by the glum look on all their faces it seems that their attempts were futile. Simpson steps out of Cherrie's house after getting her statement and pulls her thick coat around her, not bothering to push her arms through the sleeves.

"Cherrie's calmed down. Said it gave her quite a scare, the look on his face. She knew Clara was in trouble."

Dawson nods sadly and continues to stare at the puddle to his left, reflecting the blue lights.

"Sir?"

"Yes. Good work, Simpson."

"Are you okay?"

Dawson bites his bottom lip for a moment before finally looking Simpson in the eye.

"How could I have been so stupid?"

"Sir?"

"All the signs were pointing towards Kane, and I just ignored them."

Simpson sucks her lip and averts her eyes, gazing around at the circus of people. Whether she's too polite to say '*I told you so*' is unknown to Dawson, but he silently thanks her regardless for her discretion. That's when Dawson sees Roberta Holmes hurrying up the street towards them. Dawson rolls his eyes and makes towards his car.

"Take care of her, Simpson, would you?"

CHAPTER 65:

He's almost sure it was him. Pursing his lips and retreating his steps, he leers between the alleys as he marches back towards the station wondering where he could've gone.

Rong Valley Train Station is not unlike your typical English rundown drop-off. Behind the commuters are flaky tiles on the walls, distorted announcements on the tannoy system and the walkways and lifts that seem to always smell of piss. Rong Valley Station is no different, except it only has two lonely platforms joined by a solitary bridge that looks like it could collapse any minute.

He dodges the oncoming traffic of people fresh from the Northern line from Chester and jogs up the stairs to the bridge two at a time. Making his way safely onto Platform 2, he has a better view. Glancing up and down and between the windows of the stationary train, despite knowing that the 14:31 to Bradford won't be leaving for another 23 minutes.

Shrugging and deciding to give up, he pushes open the door to the toilets. Needless to say, the sheet on the front door saying that these had been inspected by staff just over a half hour ago was wrong. He crinkles his nose at the smell, the overflowed sink and the wet, used paper towels uncharitably discarded on the filthy baby changing table. He seems to be alone once a man in a smart suit steps out of a cubicle and coughs awkwardly before fixing his tie and stepping out without washing his hands, his suitcase clanging off the wooden threshold, making it splinter and fall to the already unswept floor.

As he proceeds to the urinal, halfway through emptying his bladder he hears the sound of a phone vibrating viciously, before cutting off. Looking into the grimy mirror in front of him, through the obscene racial and homophobic graffiti directed at some poor boy called Malcolm, he sees that the second cubicle is in use. Shaking the residual urine from himself, he crosses to the sink and washes his hands noisily. Opening the door so the creaks ricochet around the grubby bathroom, he lets it slide closed and waits for the thud as it hits the frame. Holding his breath for good measure, he only has to wait seconds before a voice thunders out of the cubicle, almost making him jump in fright.

"Lee? Yeah, I'm in the train station now. I'll need you to meet me in Long Buckby with the remaining tickets. Scumpy could only get me that

far on such short notice... Great, cheers mate...
Oh, you know, hiding out in a fucking toilet
cubical... 'cause Dawson has taken over my house
and I'm sure I'm plastered all over the news by
now... Must've been Donna the slut. I'll be sure
that my boys find her, the rat. She'll pay for what
she did to me. I'll tell you-"

The door of the bathroom jerks open with a
painful screech and a man wearing thick glasses
apologises to him as he shrinks off to the urinals.
Stepping out onto Platform 2 again, he hurries
forward, bringing his phone out of his pocket in
the process. It *was* him!

CHAPTER 66:

Kane curses silently before hitting the red '*end call*' button on his emergency phone. He glares around at the phone numbers requesting sex and defaming members of the community and feels like kicking the barriers surrounding him down. Kane Yates. Forced to sulk in a fucking toilet cubicle for over an hour because of some woman. His blood hasn't stopped boiling since he got the call from Matty earlier. His fucking *wife!* If he got his hands on her now he wouldn't tire from beating seven shades of shit out of her. But he has to remain focused. His anger will make him sloppy. He can't lose focus until he is at least on the plane at Gatwick.

Who knows who the coppers have told? He doubts the airports have been notified just yet... But trains get delayed and life happens. He glances at his watch for the fourth time in a minute and shuffles around the tight cubicle. He has never felt claustrophobic before, but being stuck in this cell has brought out a new side to him. He imagines himself in a movie. Standing still whilst the world goes on around him.

BRADD CHAMBERS

Countless bodies coming in and out of the bathroom. A quick rest stop before their resumed commute. Sped up as his clock ticks slowly. He wonders if the audience would sympathise with him. Or would he be the big bad dad who killed his daughter?

45 minutes before his train is due to arrive he gasps in fear as the door to the bathroom is aggressively opened with shouts announcing the arrival of police. He curses and looks around him aimlessly, knowing he has no means of escape. Then glancing above, he climbs desperately onto the slippery toilet seat and pushes open a slate on the roof. Luckily, it gives way easily and he finds himself trying to crawl up into his hiding place, closing his eyes against the harsh collection of dust, dead insects and God-knows-what-else attacking his face. But before his legs have crossed the threshold of the hole, he's being dragged down by armed officers roaring in his ear about being under arrest and having the right to remain silent.

CHAPTER 67:

"Robby, please! Take me with you, *please*!"

Tears slide down Roberta's cheek as she watches Lydia being stuffed into a silver car by a flustered looking social worker. It takes all of her energy not to reach out to her. When the door is shut, she sees her little hands clasp at the window before being driven off promptly.

"And there's no way she can come and stay with me?"

The social worker raises her eyebrows again and coughs awkwardly.

"I'm sorry, Miss Holmes. But until we do further investigations into your home life, I'm afraid we can't. Of course, it would be an ideal situation for everyone, but we have to think of what's best for Lydia."

"*I'm* what's best for Lydia. You just heard her crying out to me. Look, I've been in her position. I know how scary it is."

"Then you'll know that we're doing all we can to help her. It's a messy situation."

Roberta sulks before nodding, knowing that she's right. The social worker gives one last sympathetic smile before crossing the street to her car.

"You!"

Janine pulls herself away from the summoned police officers and charges towards Roberta, before being restrained again by a female officer about to return to the station.

"Mum, I warned y-"

"Don't you dare call me that name, you bitch. You're no daughter of mine."

The female officer finally manages to lead Janine back into the house as Ian slumps in the front doorway, too high to assess the situation. When he wakes in the morning to find that one of his only forms of income is gone, he'll be in a similar state as Janine.

"Babe?"

Roberta turns to see Jeff jogging down the street, his suit starting to darken with the dampness of the rain. As he reaches her, she finally erupts. Wrapping both arms around his neck, she drops the handle of the umbrella until it's body engulfs their heads, giving them what little privacy they have in the dire situation. After a few moments, they pull apart.

"You did it?" Jeff's eyes expand.

"I did it."

"Oh, Rob," he pulls her into another hug, his voice muffled by her hair and her coat. "It's for the best. You know it is, right?"

Roberta hates to admit it, and it makes her sob even more, but she nods her head, too physically drained from the past few weeks to argue any longer. She just hopes that Lydia won't hate her.

CHAPTER 68:

"I don't fucking believe it."

Dawson sits in his office with this morning's Herald spread over his desk. His mouth is agape and he's gobsmacked at the headline.

'*Detective Inspector Dawson Fails To Cover Up Cousin's Murder.*'

As he turns to the inner pages for the whole scoop, his disgust grows as he reads the fabricated details of the case. How the force doubted Kane from the start. How Dawson chose to ignore the warning signs. How he was chasing dead ends in the hope that public interest and funding would drop to zero. And right in the centre of page 4, around the edges of a pristine picture definitely taken from a few years ago, was a full exclusive interview with DS Jade Simpson.

Grabbing the paper and scrunching it up with a balled fist, Dawson marches down the corridor, ignoring the stares from his colleagues and the floating pages he's leaving in his wake. Slamming down the article on Simpson's empty desk, he prepares to scream at her until the frames fall off the wall. But just as he intakes his breath for the first shouting match, he pauses. The walls are already bare. In fact, the only thing in the office, spare of the desk and chair, is Simpson herself. He grins.

"Looks like my work here has already been done. Fired, I presume?"

Simpson cocks her head to the side with a slight smirk.

"On the contrary *sir*, if I was a betting woman, I'd put money on you being fired."

The flame erupts from Dawson's eyes.

"Now, you list-"

"No. You listen!"

Simpson slaps her hands off the table and stands, hovering over Dawson in her six-inch heels.

"You made a dog's dinner of this investigation as soon as you let Kane Yates leave the morgue the day we found Jill's body. I told you countless amount of times of my conspiracy, but you chose to ignore it. Too busy being bound by blood. Well, let me tell you Dawson, I was right. Wasn't I?"

Dawson glares up towards her.

"What the hell do you want, Simpson? My job?"

"Your job?" she laughs. "Your job! Do you really think I wanted *this* job? Lapping around like your puppy all these years. Laughing at your jokes, bringing you coffee. And for what? A pathetic drug dealer too stupid to know that we can see that he's growing weed in his attic from our heat sensor? A kid that has too much juice and starts throwing punches on Chessington Street? No, I'm better than that. Finally, a fucking murder case. My time to shine. And I spot the culprit a mile off, but because you're Captain Big Bollox you get to call the shots? Fuck that."

She starts chuckling, her eyes wild. The silence is broken a few moments later when Dawson spits through gritted teeth.

"How long?"

She smiles again.

"Excuse me, *sir?*"

"How long have you been planning this?"

"Well, there was nothing planned, actually. I guess I started to hate you around about Christmas two years ago. Remember? That time I told you the kid would be under the bridge. Where all his friends said he liked to hang out. But no-o-o, you ignored me. Got all the drug dens and halfway houses checked out before, bored of playing hide and seek, the kid finally returned home. We could've found him, but you were too arrogant to listen to other people's opinions.

"After that, you angered me even more as the weeks went by. I started looking for other jobs. Anywhere but here. Fresh out of the academy, I jumped at my first shot as a copper. But Rong Valley? Please. Even my old Sargent asked why I was moving here. I got a few offers, but nothing that paid as well, and some would've bored me to tears. Then, just last week, I got an interview with Manchester Metropolitan Police. Detective Inspector role. Found out yesterday that I got the job, in the middle of all that carnage. Just when things were starting to get exciting. A man on the run, I love a good goose chase."

"And Roberta Holmes?"

The cackle that comes from Simpson sounds like a completely different person.

"Oh, that was easy. We met one time on Promised Hill. The homeless man that died of pneumonia, if my memory serves me well. We got chatting and she offered to take me for a drink. All confidential, of course," she raises her eyebrows in a humorous way. "Then, after that, she kept popping up. We formed a sort of alliance. She'd let me know of the goings on in the underground scene, and I'd let her in on what I could on our end."

"So, all this time… This whole investigation. Those awful stories… It was you," Dawson narrows his eyes, too depressed to be angry.

"Well, I didn't *always* naturally give over the information. I mean, if I shooed her out of a room, there was no stopping her eavesdropping in on the conversation. Perfectly legal, isn't it?" she smiles again. "But, yes," she examines the scrunched up half a paper that still lies on her desk. "I must say, probably some of her finest work. And that picture, it just brings out my eyes, doesn't it?"

There's that cackle again. She lifts her coat from behind her chair and crosses the room, leaving Dawson staring at the place where she stood. As she passes him, she leans in until her mouth is inches from his ear.

"Oh, and by the way *sir*, the Superintendent wants to see you."

CHAPTER 69:

The wine is sweet, but it isn't the fifth glass that is giving Roberta the bitter taste in her mouth and feeling in her stomach. Kim from PR has just left, reiterating multiple times about what time she has to get up at to get the kids to school and get into work before 9am. Whether she was hinting for Budds to offer her a lie in, Roberta wasn't sure. Considering that Kim did nothing to impact the outcome of the success of this morning's paper, short of organising a few interviews with the local football team, which was plugged on the back page. However, the whole town couldn't be less interested in the back pages. For today anyway. It was the crime and news team who were being celebrated tonight. Once Kim swings the door shut, it leaves Budds and Roberta alone together.

"Thought you'd be runnin' back to that fiancé of yours?" Budds grins, one eye closed to focus on her.

She shifts awkwardly in her chair.

"You two have a falling out?"

"No, no. Nothing like that. I just don't want to go to bed yet."

She can't imagine the pain she'll feel when she's left alone with her thoughts. The image of Lydia's hand against the car window still etched on her brain and will probably be haunting her dreams. She didn't sleep last night and she guesses a few more restless nights loom in front of her.

"Come on, we should be celebrating," Budds grins, waving at the staff that they'll take another bottle of Merlot.

That's when the door to the pub swings open and in walks Detective Inspector Donald Dawson. Roberta stares open mouthed, and turns to see Budds' reaction. It takes him a while longer, before both eyes open in amusement.

Dawson marches over to the bar and hops up on one of the stools. Pulling out his phone, he sees three missed calls from Helen, and several texts from Alicia. He opens the first one.

'Daddy, Carl has texted me saying you need to speak to me.'

He winces before scrolling through the rest.

'Daddy, I'm scared. What's happened?'

'Are you okay? Dad?'

Sighing and lifting his pint to his lips, Dawson puts his phone away, not yet ready to deal with this new development. He had left the station earlier to be greeted with Carl. With the way he was feeling, Carl was lucky he didn't get a slap in the mouth. He had tried negotiating with the DI. It seems that it is, in fact, Alicia that he is after. The thought of his crumpled tracksuit bottoms being in Dawson's house again made his already sick stomach churn. He told him to leave him alone and he'll contact him tomorrow. Had a lot on his mind. But Carl had threatened to tell Alicia that Dawson had blackmailed him into leaving the house that night. That he was the reason for the breakdown in the relationship. He thought he had a hold over Dawson, and if the detective is being honest with himself, he guesses that he does. But that's a matter for another day.

The Super had been as polite as she could be, given the circumstances. He claimed his innocence, that he obviously had no idea about Kane's guilt until Donna's confession and didn't know Kane's whereabouts until Carl and Darren Ward rang them in. She agreed that Simpson had royally fucked them over and it would be a while before the name of the station would be untarnished. So she advised Dawson to go on paid leave until the dust is settled. He could still lose his job over this, never mind being the laughing stock of the whole town. It's no wonder he's already ordering his second round.

Melting in his misery, it's a few seconds before he realises that someone's by his side. Waiting for the chuckles or the torrent of abuse, he's surprised to see Roberta Holmes goggling at him.

"Don't you think you've done enough?"

"My editor would like to buy you a drink."

"Buy me a what!"

"A drink."

"Tell him I don't want one. But I'll have another job if he's got one hanging around."

Roberta gulps.

"Have you been…"

"No. But as good as."

"How do you mean?"

"I'm on paid leave for the foreseeable future."

Dawson thinks this is the first time he's seen Roberta look uncomfortable, which gives him a small tinge of happiness. Delighting in other's misery. Typical humans, eh? He thinks to himself.

"Please come over, we'd like to talk to you."

Dawson grumbles as he lifts his pint.

"I don't want your apology," he says, joining the pair at the corner table.

"Good. We aren't going to be offering one," Budds has sobered up a touch.

Dawson stares at them blankly. If they didn't want to apologise why did they call him over?

"We want to talk," Budds leans forward, almost as if he can read his mind, "I feel like we could come to some sort of arrangement."

"Arrangement? It's a bit too late for that, now isn't it?"

"We'd like to hear your side."

"Sod that."

"Excuse me?"

"You'll just twist it again."

"I think you'll find that our paper does not '*twist*' anything. Our reporters are ethically trained. If you're in a hump because of this morning's edition, I think you should take a closer look at what were quotes from your own DS."

"She isn't my DS anymore."

Roberta looks crestfallen.

"Did she... Get fired?"

"No. She got a new job. Up in Manchester."

"Well," Budds continues, "As mentioned, we didn't print anything out of order. Those were DS Simpson's opinions. Whether people choose to accept them as their own is a different story."

"I'm not sure it's a good idea. Especially with the way my situation is on the force at the moment," Dawson stares into his emptying pint glass.

Roberta leans forward, almost touching the DI's hand before thinking better of it. This isn't some source where she can butter them up. This is the Detective Inspector of the police force.

"We want to hear your side," she says, "I'm sure the public will too."

"I should sue you for defamation," he spits towards her. "You had a little spy in the station. Are you licking around me now that she's gone?"

"No, sir. I'm not. I didn't even know she was gone until you just told me," Roberta leans back, clearly hurt.

"Look," Budds takes over again, "think about the interview. But if not, we want someone on the inside, and I'm sure you'll want the press on your side. We could work wonders together. Just have a think about it, yeah?"

Dawson doesn't dare to look either of them in the eye. He doesn't take his gaze off the beer mat he's currently tearing to shreds before he nods petulantly.

"Right. Well, I think I've had a bit too much wine. Will have to leave my car at the office and get a rather hungover taxi in tomorrow," Budds slides across the bench until he steps out, adjacent to Dawson. "You know where to find us."

Smiling at Dawson, Roberta joins her editor as they leave the pub. Dawson traipses over to the bar and pours the residual beer into his fresh pint, before slugging a good half of it. Propping himself back on his original stool, he folds his arms and stares at the blank wall in front of him. What a shit storm this turned out to be. And it's nowhere near finished. He has some serious damage control to take care of.

CHAPTER 70:

Stepping out of the McDonald's and hopping in her car, Roberta desperately tries to jerk the car awake and swivel around the corner to a neighbouring desolate street before the tears threaten to choke and blind her. There she sits for what feels like hours, but can't be more than a few moments. She screams and shakes the steering wheel in frustration. Finally, when the fog has lifted from her head, she dries her eyes with the back of her hand and scurries into her bag for a few make-up wipes.

Not bothering to reapply anything, she steps outside naked-faced and locks her car. Travelling down the street on foot, she knows if she turns right she should be on the road that leads to the side entrance to the park. With the sun beating down on her, she takes off her light jacket and hugs it close to her, deciding to take a little trip into the greenery.

May had brought a fresh rush of flowers, wildlife and the inevitable giggling of children as they run across the grass towards the play area.

Roberta clicks her heels along the dirt path and sighs, looking around at all the happy faces.

Jill Yates is nothing but a memory now. It has been six weeks since Kane was sentenced, and no matter who she spoke to, she couldn't track down Donna. Dawson was no help. Since being reinstated last week, he kept his promise in sorting a form of alliance with the press, and Roberta and Budds especially. So far, he had leaked the name of a local drug dealer who was doing the rounds in Bar Boss last weekend, but he wouldn't tell them how he got the heads up about what this Carl Hales was up to. And he won't tell them where Donna is. In fact, since giving the exclusive to the Herald about his position in the investigation, he hasn't so much as mentioned anything about the case.

She saw the girl, Clara, a few weeks ago when Roberta was entering the children's home at the bottom of Promised Hill. She was sitting at the top of a small, plastic slide and gazing out as if in a trance. Roberta had gone over to try and talk to her, but she wouldn't respond. The social worker told her not to take it personally, she hasn't spoken to anyone in weeks. The same can be said about Lydia.

Roberta has been so lost in thought, she doesn't realise how far deep into the woods she is until she sees it. Her childhood oak tree, graffitied over with fading purple paint since the last time she saw it, but still unmistakeable. With a sharp intake of breath, she shuffles off the path and over the grass to accompany it. It stands solitary in the middle of a slope down to the river, hunched over from the years of harsh wind. She has no idea how it's hollow on one side, whether it was due to weathering or man, but it's just as she remembers. Getting onto her knees, she can just about fit her head and one shoulder through now, but bringing out her phone she shines the screen onto a space above her head. And there it is. Her initials. '*RH.*'

She had etched them on here when she was younger. When she used to climb in and hide from the world. Whether it was an argument with her parents, or with a foster carer, or if the world was just feeling that little bit hard, she always ran and came to this same spot. Night or day. Groaning and pulling out of the alcove, she turns and falls onto her bum, pulling her legs up to hug and gaze downhill at the stream. Closing her eyes and pressing her face into her arms, focusing all her attention on the sounds, she could be back there. Twenty odd years ago, with the sound of the stream overhead and her hiding place sheltering her from a storm. But no matter how hard she wishes, she can't go back. She wonders if Lydia has a safe haven like she did. She hopes so, remembering the familiarity she felt when she finally broke through the trees and saw this wooden refuge waiting, attentive and alert, ready for her latest rant or sob.

She had just come from a formalised and arranged dinner meeting with Lydia. Her foster father was there, two tables away with another child, whether his or not Roberta didn't care, she just wanted to see Lydia. But, despite it being the third attempt at contact and no matter how many times Roberta pleaded or apologised, Lydia just stared into her pot of ketchup, dunking the chip in and out rhythmically. When she was safely in the car with the other child, Roberta had begged the man to speak with her.

"I don't know what to say," he shrugged, not stopping for chit-chat as he walked around his car to the driver's side, "she's fine with us."

Tears sting at Roberta's eyes once more, and she lets them slide down her warm face. They aren't angry tears like before, but sad ones. They fall silently, her giving into them, believing she's safe in her surroundings to show the vulnerability she's held captive for so long.

BRADD CHAMBERS

More titles coming soon from Bradd Chambers:

'*Daddy's Little Girl.*'

PEOPLE ARE GOING MISSING..
BUT IT WON'T BRING HER HOME

The exciting new novel, expected next year.

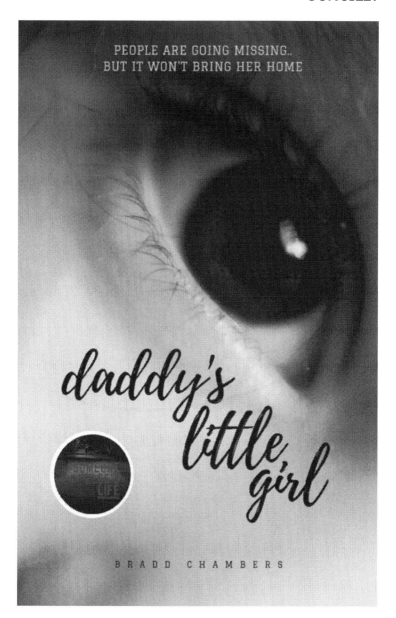

PEOPLE ARE GOING MISSING..
BUT IT WON'T BRING HER HOME

daddy's little girl

BRADD CHAMBERS

BRADD CHAMBERS

About the author:

Bradd Chambers grew up on the outskirts of Derry~Londonderry in Northern Ireland. From a young age, he started reading and writing stories.

He exceeded in English at school, and went on to obtain an NCTJ Diploma in Journalism at his local college, before graduating with a 2:1 in the same subject from Liverpool John Moores University.

He has studied Creative Writing for years at colleges around the UK. He currently writes for several online magazines.

His first novel, '*Someone Else's Life,*' received outstanding reviews, and is available now on Amazon.

Determined to leave the poor citizens of Rong Valley be... For now, Bradd is currently working on a few stand alones.

@braddchambers

BRADD CHAMBERS

31333602R00157

Printed in Poland
by Amazon Fulfillment
Poland Sp. z o.o., Wrocław